THE WORLD COUNTERS

A POST-APOCALYPTIC STORY

BOYD CRAVEN III

To be notified of new releases, please sign up for my mailing list at:
http://eepurl.com/bghQb1

1

"Stu, how much further?" John asked from the driver's seat.

John had handed the maps over to Stu to look at. They had planned their meet up with King and Michael, and still had a few hours' drive to go.

"It looks like two hundred miles left, so the timing you figured on works out to just about perfect if we don't have any more breakdowns or run out of fuel. Or catch up with the Others."

John grinned; he wouldn't run out of fuel. They had liberated every empty jug they could find and had been filling it from fuel tanker trucks that hadn't already been emptied. They had caught sight once or twice of dust clouds in the distance. They hadn't run across the cannibals yet, but if they did... John hadn't decided if he was going to split his forces or just flat out attack them with everything they had. There was no doubt in their minds that the Others were something that couldn't be left behind. They would have to deal with them now or later.

"I'd like to catch up to them," John said, his hands tightening around the steering wheel so his knuckles popped.

"Yeah, I was listening to the radio communications and then the guys talking on Blake's channel after Rebel Radio last night," Stu said, folding the map back up.

"I know," John said, his smile gone now. "The reports are starting to pop up all over the country."

"Makes me wonder how long they've been out there. That old man said they had been waiting on Judgement. Like bad lines from a B movie."

"I wouldn't have believed it until I saw it myself," John admitted. "You heard any reports of the Caliphate in this area?"

"Nothing recent. The further north we go the more careful we'll have to be."

"That's why we're taking an alternate path—"

Abruptly, the front of the truck lifted off the ground, and the shockwave shattered the safety glass of the windshield, throwing clear pebbles of it back into the men's surprised faces. Both lifted their arms to protect their eyes, but the truck had already started to roll to the left, as the RPG had hit just the front of the truck near the driver's side tire.

John braced himself as much as he could as the truck rolled twice, and they were hit in the bed as the vehicle behind them couldn't slow in time. Both men were again thrown against their restraints, everything in the cab of the truck was now sitting on the driver's side. The engine was making a wheezing noise, and they could smell coolant, gasoline, and fire. Bloody, sore and torn, Stu was the first one to get out of his seatbelt, but fell promptly with his full weight onto John, knocking the wind out of him.

"Shhhh... You okay?" Stu asked, wiping his forehead, a red smear appearing on his hand.

"I will be when you get off of me. What was that?" John asked.

"I think we were hit—"

Gunfire started rattling, and several rounds hit the bottom side of the truck that was now facing the direction they had been going. John struggled with his harness, and as soon as it was freed up, Stu dragged the Seal by the harness strap on his vest until John started moving on his own through the busted out windshield.

"That was an RRG?" John asked, ducking low and running toward the bed where they could take cover.

"I think so—"

"Down!" Tex's voice boomed, and both men hit the deck behind their truck.

Tex opened up with an M60 he'd laid over the side of the overturned truck. He had a long belt of ammunition and was putting burst after burst down range. Return fire had everyone out of their trucks in the convoy, and those in front were returning fire to men who had been waiting for them. Another RPG was fired, and everyone, including Tex, hit the dirt. This one went long instead of short, hitting the side of the highway. Tex cried out in pain, slapping at the back of his leg before falling.

"I got you," John said crawling to him, already pulling out his emergency dressing kit from a pouch.

"I got the sixty," Stu said standing up and making sure the gun was still intact.

His shots were more suppressive in nature. Down the highway about 150 yards away, the Jihadists had set up on either side of an overpass. Some had the high ground up top, and others were firing around the concrete support columns below. He fired off another burst before he started worrying about reloading, seeing he had maybe thirty rounds left. That was when he heard John talking on the radio.

"Tex caught shrapnel. I need some outgoing mail. Yeah, I'll spot for you. Set your range 160 yards from your position, and we'll walk it in."

He knew he had to have been talking to Caitlin, the former Miss America model and Special Forces operator... and almost wife of Tex. Stu couldn't imagine her reaction to hearing that he'd caught flak. Literally.

"Incoming!" Stu shouted and pulled the M60 off the bed and dove toward the two men.

Another explosion rocked the truck near the rear tires. The tailgate came apart in shards of razor sharp metal, and a tire was flung up almost straight in the air by a quirk of physics and bad luck. John rolled over to look and saw the tire coming right down at his head and rolled over at the last second, right on top of Tex. Tex let out a groan and pushed at John just as the tire hit where his head had been. It bounced twice more before rolling to a stop in the tall grass at the side of the road, burning.

"You're awful presumptuous for a first date," Tex said with a grimace that was more smile than anything else.

"You kiss your momma with that mouth?" John asked before rolling off him.

Explosions further off caught Stu's attention, and he crawled to the side of the truck and looked over the edge again.

"How far off?" John asked, feeling for his radio.

"Go ahead twenty left five."

John radioed it in and this time, still deafened by the explosions and gunfire. They heard the thunk thunk as two mortars were fired off toward the dug in Jihadists. The first round fell short, hitting just under the overpass. The second one hit the overpass right near the concrete divider. Men clutching AK47s were flung in the air.

"Keep on it, alternate by 5 until I say stop," John said into the radio.

More than one mortar opened up. The sound of the rounds coming was short lived and didn't have the trajectory of the long-range shells, but the sound they made sounded like death incarnate. Three teams were sending rounds close to 20 a minute for almost one and a half minutes, until John called a cease fire. Deafened by the explosions and choking on the smell of spilled fuel, burning tires and other unmentionable things, Stu got to his feet with the '60 and looked through the sights over the overturned truck.

"Targets?" John asked, doing the final bit of triage on Tex.

"Nothing moving. Lots of pink and red," Stu said.

"That hurts," Tex said with a grimace.

John opened up a small pouch on his vest with a cross on it and selected a syringe. He made sure there was no air in it, then plunged it into the backside of Tex, who let words fly that were so vile that the devil himself must have been tempted to visit earth and take notes. As the morphine kicked in, his eyes glazed over slightly, but knowing it was coming, he just dug in and let the drug take effect.

"We need to move you," John said, pulling another compression bandage out, "but I ain't touching your butt."

Stu was already in action, heading toward the front, followed by Caitlin who had given her soon to be husband a quick look. A belt of ammo hung off the M60 and, although it was a heavier gun than he would have liked to hump, Stu made it. Caitlin and Stu stalked forward, making sure they had overlapping fields of fire and were joined by somebody out of Stu's sight on the median. Using hand signals, they advanced until the carnage of the mortar barrage became apparent. Body parts were scattered from both the overpass and those who sought shelter behind it.

"I've got left," Stu said.

"Center," Caitlin said.

"I'm over here," the militia volunteer said.

Stu grinned. Even though not everyone on their team had started out as a professional soldier, many of them had adapted and learned quickly. Slowly, nervously, they walked through the area where the trap had been laid, mindful of any booby traps that may have been left behind. The ground smoked in places, and concrete from the overpass littered the ground amongst the broken glass from the stalled cars.

The smell of burning rubber and fuel was almost as terrible as the bodies. One twitched and John turned a little to his right and opened up with a short burst from the M60. Caitlin had already been moving as it was part of their overlapping field of fire and had just pulled the trigger on a burst of her own from her M4. The Jihadi, who'd survived by crawling under a stalled out pickup truck, jerked as the slugs tore through him and then laid still.

"Clear?" the militia member asked.

"So far," Caitlin said firing off another three-round burst into somebody who was still clinging to life, but not for too long.

"John," Stu said into his mic, "area is clear. We may need help rolling some of the wrecks out of the way for the convoy to get through."

"I'll have a team meet you up there," John said.

"How's my husband doing?" Caitlin asked in her own mic.

"I gave him a shot. He keeps asking me to touch his butt," John said, amusement evident in his voice.

"I just asked him to hold the bandage a second," Tex slurred.

"How bad is it?" Caitlin asked.

"Medic dug out a shard of shrapnel. Mostly a cut about four inches across the butt. They cleaned it, and it's already getting stitched."

"Tis only a flesh wound," Tex said.

Stu let out a chuckle, and Caitlin snorted.

"Let's go, if we hurry, we won't be late," Stu said motioning to the man on the far side. "Let's push this to the side." He put the M60 down and leaned into a truck that had flipped. As Stu started rocking, a team came forward on double time and leaned into it as well.

They rocked the truck back on its wheels from its side. Reaching in, Caitlin made sure it was in Neutral, and they pushed it toward the shoulder.

"Now if me and John's truck was this easy," Stu said ,sweating.

"Sugar, you're going to have to find a new ride. Don't worry, you can hang back with Tex and me."

Grumbling, "That's what I was afraid of..."

2

_____

"Mr. President?"

"Yes, Patrick, come in," the president said, pushing his chair back and standing to greet his longtime assistant.

They shook and, when the chair across the desk was offered, Patrick sat. The president followed suit.

"Sir, we've just heard back from Franklin Hines."

"You mean after Blake turned down my kind offer that was conveyed through him?"

"Yes, sir, Governor Hines has once again reached out to the Homestead. He never took Blake's jibe about shelling Davis to heart and knew it was a message, not a threat... so he flew out by Huey and spoke with them face to face. Sir, Blake has fulfilled his pardon in Hines' own words."

"Patrick, that's bull. Hines needs to work harder. That right wing hillbilly needs to understand our predicament. Do you think Hines didn't properly convey the jam we're in?"

"Yes, sir, I spoke with him myself. I briefed him on the parts disruptions from Monterey, Mexico as the cartels,

North Koreans, and terrorist elements have moved through."

"And what was his answer?" the president asked.

"Sir, he said he didn't want to be governor himself. He doesn't blame Blake for wanting to be out when his terms were up. Blake Jackson will not be coming back into work as Kentucky's director of FEMA."

"This isn't something he can just deny," the president objected and waited for Patrick's response.

And waited. And waited another minute.

"I said, this *isn't something that Blake can deny*. Every facility he's gone through, every reorganization, has led to production increases in our electrical components. What he was doing, will be doing... is vital to our nation. On top of that, with the folks becoming more self-reliant, I can shift resources to those who refuse to leave the cities and to our troops who're returning home. Tell Hines that he absolutely has to move on this, and Jackson is not retired."

"Sir, I'll try, but we can't risk going in there now. There will be an open revolt, and Colonel Grady's work coordinating our troops on the ground with the new American Militia will fall apart. We can't risk that right now, sir."

"You think this American Militia is so important that I can risk being seen as a weak leader by letting some ignorant backwoods hillbilly tell me no?" the president asked, his voice rising.

"Sir, we've been together a long time," Patrick said, making placating gestures with his hands.

The president took a deep breath and then let it out slowly.

"Yes, Patrick, we have. You've stuck by my side. Is this *your* advice you're giving me, or Colonel Grady's?"

"My advice, sir. Don't force the Jacksons into a corner.

They have at least as many boots on the ground as we do, and they have the hearts of the survivors. Heck, even though he's turned the narrative around about the government being the bad guy, our image is still tarnished. There's rogue units going off the reservation, and now there's evidence coming in that elements from DHS have been working with the New Caliphate—"

"Excuse me!?" the president shouted, standing up.

"Sir, it's been in every briefing for three weeks now."

"I don't recall reading it, not once," the president growled. "Why am I just hearing of this now?"

"Sir..." Patrick said standing and pulling a folder that had been folded in half out of his inner suit jacket pocket, "Here it is," he said, pointing to a highlighted section.

"Oh, that's where our intelligence is talking about home-grown Islamic jihadists. I skip that because frankly, we all know that Islam is the religion of peace, and I'm sick and tired of these Islamophobic racist analysts insisting that..." the president caught the look in Patrick's eyes and sat down.

"Sir... Hassan has defected as feared, and there are many within the cabinet and Joint Chiefs who feel..."

"They are looking at me for responsibility? They think I let the New Caliphate in the front door?"

"Sir, you appointed him, and then remained in the blast shelter far longer than anybody predicted. There were no communications from you to anybody outside."

"A decision I regret to this day, Patrick," the president said. "When the blast went off over top of us in DC... My wife and daughters and the remaining house and senate... I didn't listen to my advisors. I didn't respond when you were trying to get in touch. My people told me that they could have homed in on my signal and sent in bunker busters."

"Sir, we still are not sure who launched on DC," Patrick said, adopting a softer tone.

"Oh, I know, but my advisors underground had most of their communications and satellite uplinks knocked out topside. Our stuff underground still worked, but we had no antennas for a bit, and our readings had showed that—"

"Sir, I know. It was a low yield, garage built atomic weapon. That's why we think it was a very old Russian suit-case bomb lost in the early Cold War, or something cooked up by the North Koreans. You would have been safe coming topside in three weeks, but it took three months..."

"Patrick, did I tell you what it was like down there?" the president asked softly, changing the subject.

"Just that you had been waiting for it to be safe to come topside, and then only after your family had a safe place to come to."

"Yes. I'll admit, I acted as a father first and president second," he said, pulling a pitcher of water from the edge of the desk and pouring two cups. Handing one to Patrick, he took a sip and continued, "Is that why there's so much distrust in me, in my policies and leadership?"

"Sir..."

"Just give it to me straight, old friend."

Patrick sighed, took a sip, and wiped the sweat from his brow. "In a large part, yes. You've refused to read any intelligence that points to Islamic terrorism from American Muslims, you've been seen to have largely ignored Israel in some folk's eyes, and you have made apologies for what we've done."

"Apologies for what we've done?" the president asked, a hint of anger in his voice.

"Sir... You're probably going to fire me for this, but

you've always wanted me to tell it to you straight. You really want to know?"

"Yes, I do. I can make that an official order if it'd make you feel better."

"Sir, you've been known as the apologist in chief for about seven and a half years now. The public perception is you've apologized to our enemies for everything we've ever done."

"America has been a bully in the world theatre! I'm just an instrument in social justice."

"And that, sir, is why you aren't trusted. You appointed Davis to Kentucky and ignored the calls when he was abusing his office. He used his troops as a mercenary squad to enrich himself and the complaints of sexual abuse were abound. Sir, I myself had my doubts about you for a while."

The president looked up and met Patrick's eyes, startled by his friend's admission.

"And what of the DHS?" the president asked, his dark pallor turning gray as the words sank in.

"Colonel Grady has ordered them to stand down. It's how we know now which parts are being directed by Hassan and the New Caliphate."

"So it is true then?"

"Sir, we don't have video, but we've had plenty of eyes on. If it walks like a duck, quacks like a duck—"

"Then it's a duck. My God, Patrick, have their stand down continue. I have a lot to mull over."

Patrick stood and offered his hand. The president rose and shook with him.

"If you see Grady around, send him my way," the president said.

"Yes, sir," Patrick said, taking the folder back and putting it in his pocket.

He started walking toward the door and marveled how much the hardened underground bunker resembled the White House. This room, for example, mirrored the Oval Office. He opened the door and, just as he was walking out, the president spoke.

"Patrick," he said, watching his old friend pause, "you're not fired. Thank you for telling me."

The door closed a little harder than was necessary. The president let out another sigh and sat back, contemplating what he'd been told.

His desk phone buzzed. He pushed the flashing light. "Yes?"

"Mr. President, a DHS company that was returning to base as ordered, has captured who they believe to be John Norton. Do you want me to have them continue to base or...?"

"Are there any interrogation assets near their location?"

"Sir, there's one we have close by labeled as a 'Trout Farm'. An Ag. testing facility, as a cover."

"Good, I want to know what Norton knows, and I need to find out how far this treason goes. Use any and all means."

"Yes, sir."

The president sat back, sighing deeply. He'd underestimated how fractured the United States had become while he had been in hiding. Underestimated it badly. One of the last communique he'd gotten out was to request an article five from NATO before things topside went dark. As much as the people felt he was guilty or shady, he knew that of anything, he was perhaps guilty of arrogance. Arrogance so deep that he'd refused to believe the writing on the wall. Arrogance that he wasn't willing to believe that, under the rules of Martial Law, large factions of those who were supposed to help... had taken it upon themselves to become defacto leaders.

Like that ignorant redneck hillbilly from Kentucky who'd had the nerve to refuse to continue helping rebuild the country. His ideas had absolutely angered him and his remaining council, but Blake Jackson's methods of getting people to work and to rebuild parts of the nation in an old world agrarian society style seemed to be working. The problem was, every time he had gotten close to finding cause to arrest or take out Jackson, his friend, or rather, Sandra's friend Norton popped up, and caused hell somewhere. The pure distrust that Norton's group had sown would come back to bite him.

The president just hoped Norton knew enough for him to use as leverage against Blake. If not, well, he still had options.

3

"We've got to take control of the drop," King told Michael. "They were ambushed. Somebody passed the word along."

Michael cursed long and loud inside the confines of the APC.

"What about the backup forces that Sandra was sending?" he asked King.

"The word is they are going to hole up and wait for us. Didn't want to send a large group our way and alert the DHS."

"Yeah, so much for their stand down order," Michael said, bristling.

They had, from a distance, watched a sudden flurry of activity at the base where the scarred man had gone. Black Hummers and transport trucks had been traveling to and fro. They hadn't gotten close to seeing if things were coming or going from the subterranean bunker, but could see many, many new faces that they hadn't seen before pulling guard duty. They both had discussed it, and their general assessment was that they (DHS) were consolidating their forces.

There had only been rumors on materials and personnel stored there, and the shady intel from the man they questioned... But they were still planning on inserting Michael as soon as humanly possible to get more intel.

"Worry later," King said as the sound of planes filled the air.

Two C130s came into sight. The sound of their engines was the loudest thing the two of them had heard other than the motor of their own vehicle. Seeing them, Michael took out a flare gun and shot off a flare. One of the planes wagged its wings side to side, and what looked like several crates came sliding out of the back of the first one. Chutes automatically deployed and the two men scrambled, trying to figure out where the loads were going to come down. They'd marked out a soybean field, the soy not quite dried out and ready for harvest.

The first plane finished, banked, and started circling away as the second plane disgorged its load. Three more chutes deployed and the plane left the same way as the first. King was already moving as the first palleted load hit the ground. He started cutting the chute away, and Michael hustled to reach another one and do the same. With the area so flat, they didn't want an errant gust of wind to potentially pick it back up.

"Sgt. Smith to Michael and King. Come in," a voice said in their ear pieces.

"Michael here," he said hitting the PTT a little harder than necessary.

"We're twenty minutes out. Do you have visual on the goods? Over?"

"You could say that," Michael said grunting as his knife parted the last of the paracord holding the chute down and heading toward the next container that landed another thirty yards away. "Yes, the load is down. Over."

"If you have to bug out, leave the orange and black striped containers. Those won't work for anybody but us. We've got some heavy shells there. Over."

Michael grinned, and King just gave him a small shake of his head. "I've got a turret to play with. How much bigger can your guns be? Over."

"Let's just say that mine is gonna be bigger than yours," Smith said, the transmission crackling at the end. "There will be enough time to measure them out if ya want, kid."

King chuckled. Michael hadn't heard him sneak up so close, but that's what the big commando had always been like. Silent as death, until he was ready to go.

"Six containers on the ground. Waiting for the other team leader and group to show up. Are you the backup that Sandra was sending?"

"Oh yeah. See you soon. Over."

"Drive safe. Over," King said, finishing the conversation.

"What is in all of this?" Michael said asking King who was working on the fasteners of the container Michael had just freed.

"Something that goes boom, I hope," King said, getting a strap off and pulling a large olive drab case down into the knee high crop next to the pallet.

Cracking the lid revealed several cases of grenades and some blocks of C4. Michael grinned, knowing how much King loved playing with this stuff. Funny enough, in the last six months, they'd blown up very little. They'd followed Blake's exploits, often retold via Rebel Radio. John's group had to get very inventive without resupply. By the looks of things, even with the four containers that weren't earmarked for Sgt. Smith's group, everyone was going to be resupplied who wanted to be - and then some.

"Oh momma, I hope you like these," King said, smiling as he pulled open a new crate. Inside were the black uniforms and tactical vests including patches.

There were a number of sizes available by the look of things, and when he held them up, Michael could see the uniform of DHS.

"A guy could get shot for wearing one of those," Michael said, grinning.

"Makes your sneak and peek a little easier."

"Do they have one in there big enough for you?"

King dug through it and made a sound as he pulled out a vest much like the one he'd been wearing with a matching shirt.

"You ain't got this by yourself no more," he grinned.

"Michael, King, this is Caitlin. How y'all doin' down there? Over?"

King's smile broke out even larger, showing the whites of his teeth.

"I thought you were gonna miss the party?" King asked into his radio.

"We got a little hung up, minor injuries, but we pushed through," a man's voice said, one they hadn't heard before, "but we should be at your location in twenty minutes."

The transmission came on the same channel that Sandra had arranged everyone to use, so without using John's name, Michael figured that they would be as vague as possible. But he did remember Caitlin and how she'd set that ambush up with the cooler of beer, and an American flag bikini...

"Head in the game," King said slapping the young man in the chest with a meaty hand.

"Good, we're ready. Securing the load now. Over," Michael told him.

"Want to get in the APC, man the turret?" King asked.

"Trust but verify?" Michael asked the big man.

"Yeah. Make sure you have armor piercing handy, just in case."

4

"Hassan, what is the delay?" Khalid asked.

"The DHS, including units loyal to me, have been ordered to report to nearest base. They now know."

"Ahhh, and how much will this set us back?" Khalid asked.

"Not as much as you think. There were only some groups that were going to fight with us. I had time to test the loyalties of many of these men, but not as many as I would have liked."

"Our Iranian and Korean friends got a little anxious. So... it is as Allah wills it. The infidels will soon understand what our calling is. Have we secured the codes to enter the other bunkers and disable their nuclear arsenal?"

"Yes, my top man himself is working with the commander of the storage bunker where units faithful to the cause are consolidating. There have been some minor complications, though."

"Minor? What is it?" Khalid asked.

"We've gotten word that Norton has been captured. His

interrogation is to start soon. We have one company of men and mixed armor waiting."

"That's *good* news, my cousin. Why wouldn't it be?" Khalid asked.

"They have mixed NATO minders working with them."

"Bah. At first chance, have them slaughter the NATO troops and take their equipment. By the time our men get to the DHS bunker, we'll all be resupplied and ready to start disarming the Great Satan. A snake with no fangs is no longer a threat. Do you agree?"

"I do, cousin. Allah Akbar," Hassan said.

"Allah Akbar. And be sure to tell me as soon as we get those codes."

"I will," Hassan said, clasping his cousin on the shoulder and then turning to leave the tent they'd set up as a temporary shelter.

The Central United States had some weird sort of pollen going on with all the unharvested crops, and the Spear of the New Caliphate was starting to get watery eyes and a scratch in the back of his throat.

5

"Blake," David's voice called.

"Hey, David, what can I do for you?" Blake replied back, static bad this time of day.

"You've got a transmission from the Governor Franklin Hines. Over."

"Can you patch him through?" Blake asked forgetting to say over.

"It's on the scramble. If you can head back in, he'd like a talk. Private like."

"Okay, I'll be there shortly. I'm working with some deplorable little beasts who are getting impatient with me anyway. As soon as I dump them..."

"Don't talk about my son that way," Sandra's voice said, cutting off his transmission.

Chuckles came out of the radio, and he looked at the thirty odd some kids he had with him on this nature walk. "I'll be in. Blake out."

"So we can get away from these mosquitos now?" an older teen girl asked him, rubbing her arms where several red welts from bites were visible.

"Dad said 'squeetos are the new state bird," Chris piped up.

The girl looked down at him, a smile tugging at the corner of her mouth. Chris was a charmer, and when he grew up, he might someday realize the effect he had on those around him. For now, he just used his powers of manipulation for evil things... like more reading time, people to play Lego, or, in this case, for Keeley, the older girl, to quit griping.

"I think they are. Your bag too heavy little man?" she asked.

"No, I'm okay. Let's go, Dad," Chris said slapping his forehead and holding his hand out to see the red smear. "It's like I'm giving blood."

Blake chuckled and wondered who'd taught him that one. The snarky girl, perhaps.

"Yeah, let's head back. All of you," he said waiting for the group to quiet down again. "Move silently as possible. Let's see if we can sneak up on a deer on the way back."

"Are we gonna eat it?" a little girl asked.

"No, but it's good practice. We did it the other day, and I want to do it again. If you can be sneaky enough to get close to a deer, you know you're moving without alerting anything nearby."

"Plus, it gets the little ones to shut up," Keeley said between clenched teeth.

Blake grinned and gave her the nod. Her face lit up, and she held a hand over her mouth to keep a giggle in. Quickly, but almost at near silence, they moved through the woods and toward the field north of Blake's homestead. After a good ten minutes of moving, they finally left the tree line and came out in the field just to the south of the old grain silo. As the last of the kids came out into the open and Blake was doing a headcount, two deer broke cover from the tall grass of the pasture and headed north along the tree line, their bounding leaps drawing everyone's attention.

"But Dad, we were quiet," Chris said.

"So what do you think gave us away? Did they see us?" Keeley asked.

"Maybe," Blake said, "but which way is the wind blowing?"

The kids as a unit started turning in place, and several stopped and pointed south toward the main body of the homestead.

"So what's that mean?" Keeley asked.

A boy named Jason, who was just a little younger than Keeley and had been vying for her attention for weeks now, had finally given up on her. He stepped up to her with a grin on his face and made a show of sniffing the air.

"What are you doing, freak?" she asked.

"Just making sure," he said with a grin, "but it was you. You smell like body spray. The deer scented us. They probably couldn't hear us, but I've been getting a whiff of that off and on now for a while."

"It doesn't stink," she said, looking at him with murder in her eyes.

"No, but if you showered more you might not have to mask the—" GAH!

The boy took off running with a furious Keeley chasing. Blake started laughing at the exchange and felt Chris's little hand in his. They both started walking as the line of kids fell into a disorganized group heading back toward the big barn in the distance.

"Dad, why is Jason mean to her, and why does Keeley always punch him on the shoulder?" Chris asked.

"I think it's because they like each other," Blake said honestly.

"You mean they like to play Legos together?" Chris asked, a hopeful note in his voice.

If he could grow his Lego playing mafia, he could soon make bigger and better structures. With the help of two big kids—

"Not like that. Kind of like how me and your mom like each other."

"Keeley's going to have babies?!" Chris asked in a horrified voice, stopping walking and pulling on Blake's arm.

"No, no... I mean... Oh jeez. I think I explained it wrong."

"Oh," Chris said starting to walk again, "want to try again?"

"Yeah, I'll have your mom explain it to you some day."

Blake grinned, knowing he couldn't pass the buck that easily, but he'd try.

"GOVERNOR HINES," BLAKE SAID INTO THE RADIO HANDSET IN the bedroom that Sandra kept for more private conversations, "what can I do for you?"

"Blake. Before I say this, I want you to know that this isn't coming from me."

Blake grunted and turned when he heard Sandra enter the room. She shot him a questioning look, and he gave her a shrug and nodded his head, indicating it was fine for her to come in.

"Any time you have to preface something like that, it's got to be bad. What you got, Franklin?" Blake asked, using the familiar name of the governor of Kentucky.

"I talked with Patrick, the president's chief of staff. He

was ordered in no uncertain terms to get you back on board."

Blake sat there, a wry grin on his face. "Why am I not surprised?"

"To be honest, I was," Franklin said, "and I want you to know that if you refuse to do this, I am not going to be involved."

"Of course I'm going to refuse, but what are you talking about, being involved?" Blake asked, a cold sweat forming between his shoulder blades, the smile gone in a flash.

"I don't know. He said the president was explicit. Basically said that you didn't have a choice in the matter. Martial law and all that."

"Blake, don't do it," Sandra said, "we need you here."

Blake looked at his wife, who was rubbing her swollen stomach. It wouldn't be too awful long now. Spring was a while off, but it was marching their way quickly. They had been discussing names off and on all fall and were still at an impasse.

"When is the president looking for me to do this?" Blake asked the governor.

"Soon. He needs help in some Western states. He specifically mentioned California and Washington. Some parts of Washington still have a functioning grid, as does Canada. If the components can be built up and the Hoover Dam is repaired, we could really get a kick start on Silicon Valley and speed our recovery."

Blake was torn. With Sandra being such a petite woman, Martha and the National Guard's medical team had warned that there could be complications with the birth. The baby was growing fast, and if he/she stayed on course, it would be well over nine pounds or ten by their best guess, something that the elfin Sandra may have a hard time with. All the stress she was already under, not to mention the potential damage that happened when she'd been tranquilized by the special ops team that had attempted to kidnap her months ago... She was scared. Really and truly scared. Not for herself, but for her baby and the quiet man who she worried would have to take on raising Chris and the baby without her if the worst should happen.

"My wife's pregnant, Franklin," Blake said, wrapping his wife in a one-armed hug and pulling her close, "and I promised her I would be here when the baby is born. We're hoping for a hassle-free delivery, but the way the baby is growing, it may have to be born by C-section early. I just don't want to risk it."

"I'm just the messenger, Blake," Hines said. "I just wanted to tell you that I wouldn't be having any part of whatever happens if you refuse. I'm sure the chief of staff or one of the president's men will get in touch with you for the specifics. I wouldn't uh... recommend *shelling* them like you jokingly told him the first time I talked to you."

"Franklin. Governor," Blake said taking a deep cleansing breath and then letting it out before hitting the PTT, "I like you. I think you're a genuinely good man. You were handed a turd sandwich when they gave you the FEMA job, with little to no room to innovate. Despite that, you did the best you could, and you never abused your rank or privilege like so many others did in the vacuum of authority. Still, I think you were missing out on something important."

"Oh yeah? What's that?" Hines asked.

"I wasn't joking," Blake said in a serious tone.

There was a long pause, nearly as pregnant as Sandra, who motioned for the handset.

"My wife wants a quick word," Blake said and handed it over to her.

She pulled away and walked to the edge of the bed and sat down, one hand rubbing at her stomach again, either from the kicks, hunger, or aches. Blake didn't know, but he watched her fondly, enjoying his wife's glow.

"Do you know who's been supplying us, Governor Hines?" Sandra asked, her voice and tone at odds with the deadly warrior that resided in her.

"Colonel Grady reinstated Joint Chief of Staff," Hines said in a near whisper, his voice almost lost over the static of the transmission.

"Good, I wasn't sure if that was known to you or not. Do you know why he was able to get us resupplied when the president was against doing so? You know how and why he changed the president's mind?"

"No, ma'am," Hines said, "but I'd surely like to know. All I've heard is rumors."

"You do realize," Sandra said sweetly, "that our organized militia and volunteer army has as many boots on the ground and nearly as much hardware as the federal government?"

"Sandra, that's... please don't tell them that," Hines begged.

"Babe, don't," Blake said, pleading.

She turned to her husband, "You took the blame for the resistance of Davis and the shelling when it plainly wasn't your fault. You reacted to a bad situation and, in most cases, it was me literally *and* figuratively who pulled the trigger. That was survival. So is this. I need you. The baby and Chris need you."

"I need you too," Blake said, getting choked up. "But we know the ego of this president. He might see this as an act of war. Civil war. Treason."

"Do you know much about the Revolutionary War?" Sandra asked.

"Just what we were taught in school. Paul Revere, the Boston Tea Party, all kinds of things. Why?"

"It took three percent of the initial population of the New World to overthrow the reign of the Monarchy and its hold on America. Is this our three percent moment? Am I being selfish?"

"No, I don't think you are," Blake said, "but maybe I can resolve this another way and still be here."

"Blake? Sandra?" Hines' voice came out of the bulky handset.

"Sandra here, discussing it with my husband."

"What, civil war? That's what you were inferring, wasn't it?" Governor Hines asked.

"If needed," she said. "You should suggest they read up on some Jefferson quotes. I know we're under Martial Law, but there's also God's law. Blake wants to help, but he has a different idea that may work for all of you."

"I told them he had offered to talk to the other governors and FEMA directors by radio. I don't know why they don't think he can't be as persuasive over the radio as he is in real life."

"It's about control," Blake told his wife, who hadn't responded yet. "If they turn this down, then we know. It's about control and who's running the show up top."

"If you want to pass along to Patrick or whoever," Sandra said, "Blake said he'll work with them over the radio, but we need him here at the Homestead, and he's had all his kidneys can take of helicopter rides from here on out. Plus, it is not safe to travel with the New Caliphate bisecting the country and taking over air force bases."

"It may not even be safe to travel that way anymore,"

Hines said, telling Sandra what she already knew, "and you know what's going on with the DHS, I assume?"

"Probably more so than you do, and remember... even though we're on scramble, we're not private. There might be ears out there, so best you don't even breathe a word more of that."

"I know, but how many of them are there, and how large are their forces? We're already looking at war on two fronts; the invasion forces and the criminals and lawless. Throw in factions of the government and if your..." his words trailed off.

"Don't say it," Sandra warned. "Nothing good can come of that if you do," she admonished.

Blake motioned for the handset, and she handed it back.

"Hines, it's me again. Listen, if those are two states that they want me to work with, why don't I get started behind the scenes on scramble. Give my radio people the frequencies and codes, and I'll get in touch with them right away. Let's get ahead of this thing, because the last thing we need is our country to fracture and break apart even more so than it already is."

"I can do that," he said after a pause.

"I'd appreciate it. And Governor Hines, how's Miss Pamela doing?"

The change in subject was deliberate, but after the incidents in the DUMB where the former aid to Davis had been attacked, she'd become the governor's go-to person, helping him ease into the transition. She had all but done Davis's job, and hadn't realized it until she had a new governor who didn't have an idea how to govern... Blake thought Davis had daughters but wasn't sure if there was still a wife or not. He'd seen the way Pamela and Hines had danced at the Homestead what felt like years ago.

"She's doing well. I think she's going to stab me in the spleen if I don't get off here soon. She says you and I are only making things worse at this point. I think she might have a point here."

"She's probably right. You know what they say, though: Behind every great man is a woman rolling her eyes— Ouch!" Blake cut off, rubbing the back of his head and turning to see a mischievous grin on Sandra's face.

A chuckle came out of the radio, "You're braver than I am. I've only heard of what your wife is capable of... Uhhh... yeah... sure, hun. Listen, I have to go. Boss says... Uh huh... Okay. Hines out."

"Blake and Sandra out," Blake said and tossed the handset onto the middle of his bed and flopped onto it crossways on his back.

Sandra was more delicate about it and laid down, her head resting on his shoulder, her body curling into her husband's as much as the baby bump would let her.

"It won't come to a civil war," Sandra assured him.

Blake hoped she was right. The fighting hadn't made it to them yet, but it was only a matter of time, and he didn't want to worry about having the federal government *and* the Jihadis coming at him.

"What about the reported groups of cannibals?" Blake asked after a moment.

"One of them started off as a cult," she said, one finger trailing his chest. "The others probably turned to it out of desperation. They force people to eat the dead. Sometimes they torture them into doing it. Deprive them of food and water. They usually break them. Once turned, they are part of the gang. If they don't turn, well... they become dinner."

"So it's like the Caliphate's mandate? Convert or die?"

"Yes," she said, not meeting his eyes.

"Do we have a plan in place for these people? These cannibals?"

Blake shuddered, his mind going back in time when he and Weston had met Patty and Neil, and the circumstances of Neil and Weston's death. That had been a crazed cannibal there. Whether insane by defect, mental illness, or some sort of prion disease that becomes common in cannibals, it was an evil so pure it made Blake hope they had a plan in place, or he might never sleep well at night.

"Good," he said, his breath catching as the fingernail kept turning circles on his chest.

6

Sgt. Smith's reinforced company and John's group both made it to the rally point at the same time. They had the coordinates and had already exchanged radio greetings and were overlooking a soybean field where a giant of a man was muscling crates off of stacks of pallets. A Russian APC had dug deeply into the soil, churning up plants with the heavy tread of its tires to make it to where it was. The back hatch was open, and a young man was unloading what looked like shell canisters into the war machine.

"That's him," John said to Caitlin. "Let's go." He put down the binoculars.

"Want us to just drive up there?" Stu asked, driving Caitlin's lead truck of her mortar teams.

"Let's double up on the little trucks and get the big Deuce and a Half down there to get containers loaded," John said, holding down the button on his radio so it was broadcast to their entire group.

"Same. Jennings, have the men set up a perimeter while we load up and get ready for a fast exfil," Smith said over the radio.

"Get down here and help me load this stuff," King complained, making his Alabama accent thicker than normal.

John hit Stuart's shoulder and motioned, and the young soldier took off, almost tossing men and women out of the bed as he bounced through the ditch and onto the mostly flat field, full of soybeans. John hadn't seen Michael in months and wanted to see with his own eyes how he was doing. His own son had finally made contact via radio and was fine. That had lessened the pain considerably, but he still felt like a second father to the neighbor kid who had befriended his son all those years ago.

King stood up, wiping the sweat from his brow. He'd already sorted what they were going to be taking in the APC, but he had been curious about the two pallets that Smith's group were getting. In theory, there was enough ammunition, grenades, and M4s to arm a rather large force, but many of them already had weapons. Some of this was overkill, and then there were the pallets Smith had told him about.

A towable missile battery, ordinance, and some old Stingers. What would an artillery company need with those? Had the Jihadis somehow gotten an air force, or were they worried about the DHS? To King's knowledge, they didn't have aircraft of their own, except for some civilian grade Helos.

"Michael?" John asked, bouncing out of the back door of the crew cab Ford they'd been riding in.

Michael paused in reloading the shelves that held the turrets' ammunition and came out with a grin bright enough to light the sky. He strode forward, bare-chested with both handguns still worn low slung on his hips. They embraced hard, and Caitlin made a sound of appreciation.

Tex stumbled out of the truck in John's wake as Caitlin and Stu exited the front seats.

"Look at them man-boys," Caitlin said with a sardonic grin.

"Look but no touchy," Tex said with a slur.

"Don't get jealous now," King said. "If ya want, I'm sure somebody will be happy to grab your butt next."

A look of horror crossed Tex's face, and he started to back up until his feet tangled and he tripped over backward into the soybean on his tush. He let out a loud groan and then tried scrambling to his feet. He went up and down and finally grabbed the bed of the truck and made it to his feet.

"You okay, son?" King asked, confused.

"He caught shrapnel to his glutes," Stu said, watching as John and Michael broke the fierce hug. "John shot him up full of morphine. Guess Tex thought it was worse than it was or John wanted him to quit crying about how bad his butt was bleeding."

"Anybody else hurt?" King asked.

"Naw, sugar," Caitlin said, "not like that. The rest was cuts 'n' bruises. Don't tell Tex, but they pulled a shard out of him this big," she said holding her fingers apart a few inches. "He's been pretending to be the black knight all the way here since. It was cute the first hundred miles," she said with a sniff.

"I'm okay," Tex said with a grin and walked up to the big man. "Good to see you again, King. Sorry, I have no tolerance to morphine, so it makes me loopy."

"Loopier than normal," Stu said.

"Hey now, watch it. Y'all don't want to get on his bad side," he said, pointing to King.

"Loopy," King agreed with a grin.

They exchanged handshakes and saw as Smith started

organizing his men to start loading up the crates King had been inspecting. After a few moments of directing them, he walked over and introduced himself to the group.

"You're what, company strength?" King asked.

"Just about. Most of us were National Guard, but we've been reinforced with Silverman's group for this mission."

"When you said you had some stuff earmarked for you, I was expecting artillery rounds. Something special. What's up with the anti-aircraft ordinance?" King asked.

"I was wondering that myself," Michael added.

John looked up sharply. "We weren't told about any air capability," he said, "has something changed?"

Smith shook his head and motioned for everyone to come in a little closer. "No, those two pallets are heading back to the Homestead. We've been waiting on a bigger resupply to get this equipment dropped to us."

"You want anti-aircraft batteries and a radar installation at the Homestead?"

"Yes," Smith said. "Ever since Boss Hogg sent the Apaches and caught us flat-footed. Also, that's what the Stingers are for. Apaches can light up the radar from afar if we leave it on, but the Stinger is a fire and forget. A few pieces will be doled out as needed, but we're hoping you folks have the goods on this DHS installation and we can get a massive resupply from there."

"You mean Sandra's man at the White House doesn't know what's inside there?" Michael asked.

"No, he doesn't. For whatever reason, the DHS was running and operated like a separate branch of the military, one that existed on American soil. It had very little oversight and a blank checkbook for years after 9/11. We do, however, know about the facility they are in and have blueprints."

Smith dropped the pack he had on and dug through for

a minute then pulled out a set of prints that had been rolled and folded to fit. It consisted of dozens of pages and was quite thick. He handed it to King who unfolded it and rolled it out, looking at the top sheet thoughtfully.

"That door is just about nuke proof," King said, "but we think we have ourselves a way in."

"Oh yeah?" John asked, "How's that?"

"With these," Michael said opening the crate he'd left outside the APC and opening it.

Black DHS uniforms, full.

"Is there enough for a full squad?" Smith asked.

"Yeah, but do we have enough operators on the level to fill a whole squad for a mission like that?"

Smith looked around and shrugged. "I'm not sure. I don't know if my men are. Most of us are volunteers or were until the SHTF," he said spelling out the letters, "besides, somebody's gotta man the big guns."

Michael looked pointedly at the line of trucks and towed artillery that had stopped half a mile back.

"I guess yours is bigger than mine," he told him with a grin.

"Don't you tell him that," Caitlin piped up. "He'll get a big ole head. Besides, I think we can handle the special ops stuff if Michael and King can fill us in on what they've been watching."

"Nuh uh," Michael said, "we're going in too."

John made a rude sound and looked away and then back at the kid. He now knew who King really was. When he'd been breaking him out of the FEMA/Jail camp, he'd had no idea that the giant of a man had been a special ops trainer, but Sandra had let him in on that fact and reminded him he'd probably run into him a time or four himself back in the day. Now, he'd been training Michael for months on end. The skinny kid who'd walked out of the Talladega National Forest with two little ones in tow was now a young man. Lines were carved into his face, hard lines from doing things no kid should have to do. Then again, he wasn't a kid any more and had turned into a very capable operator, or at least that's what John had heard.

"Okay," John said after a long pause.

"Hey, where's Linny and—"

"They're at the Homestead, sugar," Caitlin answered.

"This is our last field op," Tex said. "Me and Caitlin are going to settle down a bit. Heal up. Besides," he walked up and rubbed her stomach, "she's going to be laid up from fighting soon."

Caitlin almost popped her soon-to-be husband in the nose and instead turned it into an ear slap. Tex laughed. John turned, his mouth gaping open.

"Yeah, medics confirmed it," Tex said with a grin. "The news is almost as good as getting new guns and stuff to blow things up," then he let out a rebel yell.

After a second, it was chorused by both Smith and John's men. A smile tugged at the corners of Michael's mouth, remembering King's words about the Homestead and why it was necessary to leave when they did.

"I didn't know that's why you were switching jobs," John said. "I figured you were going to..."

"This lunkhead," Caitlin said pointing one perfectly manicured nail at Tex, "ruined my announcement. I was going to tell folks after we take down the bunker and get the absolute proof the president is requesting."

"How many men is it going to take to get that equipment back to the Homestead?" Michael asked, nodding at the different colored pallets, changing the subject.

"We're sending a short squad. They'll have friendly territory to travel through," Smith said, "and reinforcements until they get back to Kentucky. Ones who can keep quiet."

King nodded. Blake's family home had been attacked or harassed from everything, including roving gangs, thugs, criminals, National Guard units, regular military, and then Apache gunships. How it was still standing was anybody's guess, and he knew having all their artillery tasked with them would leave them vulnerable... unless Sandra had held some back. Or gotten reinforcements from somewhere else...

"How long to plan our entry?" Smith asked. "Not that I'm going in, myself."

"Let's take a day or two to figure things out," John said. "I need to study these plans, and I'm sure we have some charges to prep in advance if your door key doesn't work," he said nodding at the pile of uniforms.

7

Colonel Grady looked at the stack of papers the president had sent. He'd been avoiding one in particular, as he didn't want to take over communications and get in touch with Sandra yet. The president wouldn't act until he moved, but in the meantime, he had other matters more pressing than assuaging the ego of the most powerful man on earth. He had a chance to do some real damage to a larger force moving in from Mexico. Available air assets were scrambled, and long-range bombers had been loaded and filled to capacity with fuel.

Both North Korea and the advancing Jihadis were about to feel the wrath of the United States. The memo he had in front of him had only been seen by two other sets of eyes: the lieutenant who had brought it to him and the president. In it was a detail of the uranium used to make the crude nuclear device that had detonated in Washington DC. In it, it described how every batch of uranium had a unique quality and could be traced back to the reactors it was enriched at. This uranium had come from a reactor that the

North Koreans had just shut down within the last eight months. Add that to the fact that US Special Forces and Ops had taken North Korean prisoners working as advisors in ships attempting to land on US soil... They had all the proof we needed.

"Sir, the president has asked you to take a call from Ambassador Lin," his secretary said from the doorway to his office in the bunker.

It startled him, and he almost spilled his half-forgotten coffee on his stack of papers.

"What does he want?" Grady snapped back, wishing his tone hadn't come out so harsh.

In truth, the president or the other ambassadors were dealing with other foreign dignitaries and not men like Grady who ran the actual machinations of war. Then again, these weren't normal times, and there wasn't anything normal about these circumstances.

"Sir, the Chinese Ambassador is concerned about aircraft takeoffs on Okinawa and the USS John C. Stennis."

"Patch him through, and Celia, shut the door for me would you?" he said motioning to his open door.

This was not going to be a pleasant conversation, he mused as the door swung shut and his phone started ringing.

"Ambassador Lin, Colonel Grady here. What can I do to help?"

"SIR?" CELIA SAID AT THE DOOR A FEW MOMENTS LATER, "THE president is trying to get through to you. Both of your lines are busy."

She had opened the door a crack and saw Grady with his head in his hands. He brought them together, palm to palm and recited something so softly she couldn't hear it. His phone was lit up, all lines flashing, and after another ten seconds he turned and looked to his secretary.

"Send him to line three in a moment," Grady said. "I have to get someone off the line."

"Yes, sir, I figured it was something like that."

When the door closed, he turned and picked up the handset and hit the extension for his second line first.

"I want another air drop. We're resupplying units here," he said reading off coordinates. "Yes, I know that's Kentucky. Drop it on those coordinates, and I'll have forces on the ground ready. Yes, make the loadout what I said even if you have to borrow from other units. I know, I should have my men in Supply doing this, but this is for something that is time sensitive, and I don't have enough of it to fill out all the forms. I'll send those to you shortly. Yes, wheels up as soon as possible. Once up, radio silence until the drop is made. Thank you." Grady hung up that line and hit the button for number three.

"Sandra, listen, I know Blake doesn't want to, but he needs to know that... I know. If you're sure. Yeah, I figured as much," he said smiling into the phone. "Listen, I have a delivery inbound. Don't be alarmed. Yes, watch for chutes." He read off the coordinates and held the phone back as she cursed. "I know that's the field that Gerard's... Yes. Trust me. Yes. After today I may not be able to help you. No, I'm not doing anything stup—"

Extension two started to ring, and Celia poked her head in. "Sorry, three was still busy. The president sounds upset about something."

He waved her off and walked to his door, closing it and turning the bolt, locking her out.

"After today, nothing is going to be the same. Hunt some cover if things get too hot. I have to go. You too, kid."

He hit the button for the second extension.

"Mr. President, Grady here."

"I can't get through to my own men, how can I fight a war?" the president asked, his voice raised and higher in pitch.

"Sir, I still have Ambassador Lin on the phone. You gave the word for me to deal with him while we bomb a country on his southern border."

"He's still harping on you? Get him off the line and come to the command room."

"Yes, sir."

The line went dead. Grady hit the first extension and cleared his throat before speaking, "Ambassador Lin, listen, something has come up that is time sensitive. Can we continue this conversation in another hour or two when the current crisis has passed? No, we do not plan on entering your sovereign air... Yes, we do have flights that are passing the manmade islands... Yes, our Carrier Battle Group is near... No, sir, China has nothing to worry about. Now, if you'll excuse me. Thank you."

He hung up the phone and grabbed a handful of tissues to wipe his brow. Standing, he stretched and wondered how long it would take for word of what he'd set in place to reach the president. Would he have Grady executed? Firing squad or hanging? Detention? Gitmo? No matter what happened, his actions would give the civilian militias the ability to defend themselves from enemies, foreign and domestic. He just hoped that what he had done was enough.

"Sir?" His secretary was knocking on his door and wiggling the handle. "Sir, the president is on the line and insists you hurry up."

One of his final acts ready to execute, Colonel Grady walked to his door, unlocking it and pulling it open so fast that Celia almost fell into him. He stepped back to make sure he wasn't going to be fell upon. When she got her balance back, she stepped back, and he walked out.

"Celia. You understand a closed door is meant for privacy? That the person behind the door does not want to be disturbed?"

"Yes, sir, but the president...?"

"Yes, I am going to go deal with him, but first I have a question for you. How long have you been my secretary?"

"Sir, uh... sixteen years the first time around until your retirement. Six months now."

"And do you have another three and a half or four more years in here?"

"Yes, sir," she said, a frown tugging at the corner of her mouth on one side.

"Good, then you can draw retirement, yes?"

"Sir?"

"You've been a nosy pain in my ass. How about you put your papers in, effective today, and save me the trouble of having to fire you?"

She blanched, but his words hit close to home. She had been nosy, and it wasn't the first time he had found her lurking outside his door. Initial investigations done quietly had shown she was a spinster with no outside contact for much of her life. She was just nosy and felt the need to be in the middle of everything. Knowing he might be dead after today and finding her at his door again, it felt good. Maybe trite, but good.

"Sir?" she asked, looking around at the other secretaries who helped run the lives of the officers they worked for.

They were all staring at them both.

"Goodbye, Celia. Don't be here when I come back," he said aloud. *If I come back*, he finished in his head.

8

"Khalid, our contact in the base has the codes," Hassan said, ignoring the hustle and bustle of what was happening around him as aids and radiomen coordinated with Khalid.

"Good. Give me one moment, we are trying to—"

"Sir, Mohammad's ship has been hit as they were unloading in Mexico," one man said, running up.

"Excuse me?" he said, his voice cracking.

"Sir, they... it's a bombing run," another voice said and then went silent, holding a hand to his ear. "Multiple ships have just been sunk. No missiles, our men think there're submarines out there."

Khalid cursed. He'd banked on most of the subs being in the seas around Korea and China and the Atlantic, where the mercenary forces he'd hired had tried to land and tie up and overtax the east coast's defenses.

"If we get control of the United States Nuclear arsenal, we can stop all of this," Hassan said.

Everyone in the room went silent, and Khalid turned to

his cousin. "I thought we could only cripple their capabilities?"

"Is that even possible?" one of the aides asked, a shocked expression on his face.

"Everything is possible if you put your faith in Allah," Hassan said.

"Sir," Jamaal, one of the aides said in a hurry, running up, "the American president has just launched against our allies in North Korea. We are getting reports... Sir, I do not understand. My contact was suddenly cut off, and I cannot reach them anymore."

"It would seem to me," Khalid said looking at the stunned room, "that the Americans have started the retaliation all over again. Let us hope that most of their assets are still focused elsewhere. It won't be long before even the military that's not yet made it back to the mainland will be too late to help."

"Hassan, how long would it take for us to be ready to move on to the missile silos?" Khalid asked after a long pause.

"If you take into account the time of travel," Hassan said scratching his head, "I think we can be ready within thirty six hours, but our forces are awaiting resupply. Not all agents in that bunker are with us sir, and there is a contingent of NATO to work around. A week is more realistic."

"Sir," one of the other aides said rushing up, "more of our troops in mainland Mexico are getting bombed as well, what are your orders, sir?"

Khalid cursed, and turned to his cousin, raising his eyes and eyebrows as if to ask a question.

"There's nothing much we can do for them cousin," Hassan said, "other than have them find cover and to join forces with us as we rid the world of the great Satan."

"Where are our North Korean friends?" Khalid asked through pinched lips. "Other than a few technical units and advisors, where are their anti-aircraft batteries, what have they done other than providing us with that which we've paid for?"

"I do not have the answers right now, cousin, but we will find out." Hassan said. "They are supposed to have several ships and submarines in southern California ready to help and assist."

"Then go, find out what is happening, and get back with me as soon as you can," Khalid told him. "And make sure we can move out in less than a week. Nothing else will be acceptable."

The terrorists had overtaken a small town in Nebraska, not too far from their objective. There were less than twenty people left alive, the men murdered outright, and the rest of the residents had been given a choice: join them to convert or die. It'd been this way through much of the campaign through North America. Kelly did not expect many to go along and convert, and secretly he wasn't as religious as he let on himself... But that was the way of the New Caliphate. Surprisingly, one out of five people would join. That's how their numbers grew exponentially town by town, city by city.

Since the start of their campaign, their numbers and slowly swelled, despite the fact of the constant battles, the constant fighting, and John Norton's group harrying them on their march north across the United States of America. Once the nuclear threat was neutralized or they had control of it, Khalid had planned on expanding eastward, not wanting to cross the Rockies so close to the coming winter. Taking out the heart of America, and its most populated cities, were high on his list of things to accomplish before the snow flew.

One of the other goals he had, and it was more of a personal goal, was to find the owner of Rebel Radio. Blake Jackson, aka. Backcountry J. The man who did an hour or two a day gave hope to the remaining Americans that could tune in and listen to his voice. Khalid never missed an episode and, from a strategic standpoint, he admired how Blake was able to work with the government and FEMA to get accomplished what he had at this point. Too bad for him, Khalid's plan was bringing all that progress to a halt.

Walking out of the motel room that they'd commandeered for a command post, Khalid went to his own quarters. Instead of setting up tents, the officers had taken over a Motel 6. There was one thing the hotel had got wrong, their slogan was: "We'll leave the lights on." But how could they? The New Caliphate, with one stroke, had turned the United States of America into a third-world country and plunged them over 200 years back. Disease and starvation were his biggest partners in this campaign, but a little fear... Those were things he could help with. Those were what he was going to leverage to finish off the heart of the American spirit.

"Sir, I cannot reach our contacts in Pyongyang," a frantic aide said, running in with a sheaf of papers.

"Let me see what you have..."

9

"... Excuse me? Col. Grady did what?" the president asked into his red phone. "Is the Colonel available? Well, he hasn't made himself available to me yet..."

The president hung up the phone softly and sat at a perfect replica of the Resolute desk, which resided at the White House in the Oval Office. He put both hands together, his fingers steepled under his chin, which rested on his thumbs. Closing his eyes, he leaned forward, thinking deeply. Questions swirled through his mind, answers were elusive. Why would Col. Grady send anti-aircraft batteries, missile batteries, and enough resupply, to Kentucky? What did Col. Grady know that he hadn't let the president know about yet? Even more important, in whose interests was Col. Grady working for?

The big question, the one that had been keeping the president up with his stomach churning in nausea close to the surface, was one he was afraid to ask himself: was Patrick correct? Was the public's perception of the president so bad that they were misunderstanding him? Or was he misunderstanding his own motives? His entire life, from community organizing through college, Senate, and now the presidency, had been about helping people. Yes, his views were controversial, especially for social justice and his economic policies. None of that mattered any more, though, because what was left of the country was largely in shambles and, to be fair, he didn't see who other than the jihadists really wanted it.

A crisis in faith? A crisis of faith in himself? He reached for his other phone.

"Yes, can you find me Col. Grady please? He is? Good."

The president waited a few moments, and there was a knock and his secret service detail opened up the door and Col. Grady walked in. The secret service agent looked at the president questioningly to see if he was needed, but the president shook his head no. The Colonel approached the desk as the door was shut behind him.

"Take a seat, Colonel," the president said.

"Thank you, sir. I was just coming to see you as a matter of fact," Grady told him.

"Yes? Was it in regards to the supplies you sent to the Homestead, Kentucky?"

"Yes, among other things, including your order," Grady said with a slight frown marring his features.

"Well, okay then. Why did we send the supplies there when they could be used closer to our coastal cities? You have to understand how this looks from my perspective... knowing how well you know Sandra Jackson and have been pressed back into service. So what is it, old friend?"

"You're under the assumption that I did something wrong," Grady said sitting forward, his posture alert but relaxed, "but there could be nothing further from the truth, Mr. President."

"Enlighten me," the president said, willing to give him

the benefit of the doubt for the moment, his own questions still swirling through the murk of his insecurities.

"The forces of the New Caliphate have dug in hard since we've started our bombing run on the forces coming through Mexico. Suddenly Pyongyang has gone silent, and they are only going to dig in for so long. Instead of attacking and destroying air bases and materials, how long until they get pilots of their own? How long until somebody gives them access codes to a silo—"

"They cannot launch nor detonate any of our nuclear arsenals," the president interrupted.

"Not directly, but what if, say... they dismantled a warhead? Rewired it to command detonate, or even made one hell of a suicidal dirty bomb? What if they were to access a silo and start feeding the air force commanders of our nukes false information? It can neutralize the biggest deterrent we have left."

"What does this have to do with sending anti-aircraft supplies to Kentucky?"

"Sir, when they get air support, and I'm sure they will... It is my belief that they will push east before taking on the westernmost states."

"Is that a guess, or do you have specific intelligence?" he asked, his face pale from the stress and anxiety.

"A little of both. Radio intercepts, half decoded messages... and sir, Blake and Sandra's homestead has become the center of the civilian militia. Unless we get the rest of our troops home and I mean *fast*, they are the only ones with enough of a ground force to even attempt to slow, if not stop, the invasion."

"You think a bunch of rednecks and hillbillies can stop soldiers? You think they can stop the New Caliphate?"

"Sir," Col. Grady said a little miffed at his casual

dismissal of the militia, "who do you think makes up the majority of the New Caliphate? Poppy farmers, goat herders, Kenyan dissidents who are looking to expand their view of Sharia—"

"Tread very carefully," the president growled, his voice low but carrying more menace than any other time the colonel had heard him speak.

"Sorry, sir, I forgot about your father... I meant no disrespect. But yes, I think these 'rednecks and hillbillies' as you call them, can and will be essential to the survival of our nation. If that means giving them the capabilities of defending themselves and helping them become more effective... I mean, sir, that's the job you brought me back for. To coordinate with the civilian militia and get some organization going."

"I didn't tell you to put a special forces operator who's so code worded I can't even see her entire file in charge of all this hardware. And her husband... On an open channel... He threatened Franklin Hines with shelling him and his position if he forced Blake to come back as ordered. This... No, Colonel, this cannot stand. I won't let this..."

"Sir, you obviously disagree with what I did and why. Could you please explain to me why so I might better serve the office of the President of the United States of America?" Col. Grady asked.

He was careful with how he worded things. He'd slipped up on the Kenyan dissident thing... it hadn't been directed at the president, but at the tip of his tongue as one of the last things he'd read after firing Celia. The overall makeup of the forces they were looking at... Because the only North Koreans left alive were the ones not in North Korea, or in their underground bunkers. It'd be too hot for them to come out for decades, and China was already blowing up the phone numbers of every remaining government official in the USA about the use of nuclear weapons. Even South Korea, who had remained out of the fight, had become belligerent, knowing the radiation and fallout would also affect them as it would North Korea's northern neighbor.

"The office of the president? Is that some careful way of saying you support the chair but not the man sitting in it?" the president asked, his voice back in that low growl.

"Sir, I support the president of the United States. I support the Constitution, and I have always upheld my oaths, whether retired or not, sir."

The president stared at him for a long moment.

"What did the Jacksons say? Is Blake going to get back to work as directed?" the president asked Col. Grady, guessing one of many reasons for Grady's special drops.

"At this point, he is not willing to risk air travel with the New Caliphate bisecting our country. Even with our Air Force and Naval assets that are now in position on the west coast... it's still risky—" The Colonel held up a placating hand when it looked like the president was about to erupt in a fountain of blood from his head exploding he went on, "but he did say he would be in touch through scrambled transmissions to both Governors and FEMA directors. As you know, California is a complete mess, and what forces we have there are keeping the grid safe in Washington state."

"So he didn't say no?" the president asked.

"No, sir, he offered a different solution to the same problem. I'm sure that once travel has become safer and his wife gives birth, he'll be more able to consider a position that requires him to be more... mobile."

It was only a partial lie, but one Grady gladly told. The president had never liked the Jacksons, especially after shelling Davis, whether it had been justified or not. For whatever reason, the political fallout of the UN/NATO troops John Norton had fought had fallen on the president as well. He was tired of being belittled, pushed around, and looked down upon. His own biases and prejudices had finally surfaced when there were no more TV cameras to record him in his true self. Still, Grady reasoned, there was always a good explanation he could offer the president for why he'd given the Homestead the ability to defend itself from its own government.

"Has he already started?" the president asked, his face stony now.

"Yes, right after Governor Hines got back in touch with him."

"And have you been in touch with him since?"

"Blake? No, Mr. President, but I have been in touch with Sandra." Which was true, and the records would show that. If there was a recording, well... he was as careful as he could be, and if it got out, he'd either live or die by the consequences of his actions. "She's coordinating a push that sweeps from the south and cuts the supply lines from Mexico. Our bombers and subs have decimated the ships bringing in men and supplies, but there is still a large stockpile in Mexico. With boots on the ground, we hope to cut them off."

"Have you heard from the Mexican ambassador yet? I haven't heard anything from them since the bombing on their coastline."

"Their ambassador is dead, sir. Three weeks now. They have less of a government than we do at this point," Grady said, and mentally winced. "With no more war on drugs and no one to purchase what they have, the cartels have gone after the only other thing they think they can profit from."

"What's that?" the president asked.

"Power. It's almost feudal there. Each of the major cartels has taken control of areas of Mexico. The remnants of the Mexican Army have either fled or joined up with the cartels or Jihadis."

"So let's get back to Kentucky," the president said, steepling his hands and resting his chin on his thumbs again, staring at Grady who was starting to sweat from nerves. "Sandra Jackson, by your own admission, directs and, in effect, controls the largest ground force in the United States of America. Somebody that we have been trying to bring into the fold, control or whatever," the president said, making a dismissive hand gesture. "Her husband outright spread dissent when they coordinated the FEMA breakouts in Alabama, Georgia, Louisiana and a few other states from what I read...

"And I am urged to go easy on these folks. Then..." The president's voice had been growing steadily louder, "...they shell a government official. Right or wrong in his actions, they have done their damndedst to make the government out to be the bad guys, with no fear of retribution. Hell, our response to make Blake FEMA Director of Kentucky worked, and I hated it. Now you are giving them weapons and armament that allows them to fend us off, should we need to stop them from forming their own central government?"

The last was almost shouted. This was what Col. Grady had been waiting for. He merely shrugged his shoulders, his face impassive, though the sweat betrayed how nervous he was.

"Well?" the president asked him pointedly.

"Well what, Mr. President?"

"You have nothing to say to that? You went outside the

chain of command and armed what I believe to be terrorist elements within our own government—"

"Excuse me, SIR," Grady shouted, losing all sense of composure. "The only terrorists within this country working against the government were appointed by *you*, sir. You have done nothing but tear our country apart for seven and a half years."

The president was gaping, his jaw almost dragging on the desk he was so surprised.

"Furthermore, SIR," Grady shouted, "those rednecks and hillbillies in Kentucky have put themselves out there time and time again. Not only do I know those rednecks and hillbillies personally, but they are also doing a better job of rebuilding this nation than you are, sir. You've been nothing but a sniveling, corrupt community organizer who's been hell bent on turning America into your version of a Saul Alinsky's UTOPIA. You followed every RULE for Radicals and were surprised when the country fell? Sir, you are not only ignorant, you are stupid if you don't believe people have seen what your 'leadership' has brought us," Grady said, almost foaming at the mouth.

Months and years of the administration had been grating at him. He'd seen the military gutted, Americans spied upon... The president giving orders to have Americans killed in drone strikes... directing the Supreme Court to interpret the Constitution to fit his agenda and, when that didn't work, writing executive orders to force his wants and vision of the country to become a reality.

"Your deal with Iran all but *guaranteed* that they would start uranium enrichment. Your failure to even read or say ISLAMIC Terrorism or anything to do with it, gave our enemies breathing room to make a deal with North Korea—"

"Col. Grady," the president shouted, interrupting the diatribe.

"Sir," Grady said after a long deep breath.

"You will show me some respect when you are in my presence. Your insolence insomuch—"

"I respect the office of the president. You, sir, I have none for."

"Really?" the president said, his face pale and gray.

"Sir, you'll be remembered as the man who killed Osama Bin Laden, unleashed nuclear weapons once again, and the man who brought about the destruction of the United States."

"You're relieved of duty," the president said in a quiet voice, his hand massaging his chest.

"Sir, I was pressed into duty after I retired. It was your choice to force me back. So yes, I armed our best hope of defeating the invaders. If I have to quit again, well, that won't be so bad. I have a place to go and hide out the aftermath."

"Aftermath? You think I'm going to let you get away with this so easily?"

"Sir, even now, the Chinese are scrambling a response. You were warned, sir. Whoever replaces me will have to deal with the fallout, whether it's conventional or nuclear."

"I had the ambassador's call sent to you to diffuse the situation." The man seemed to almost crumple within himself as he sat back on the desk, a defeated man.

"Sir, this is war, and you micromanaging it is going to cost a lot of lives. I'm going to take mine and hunt a hole now that you've relieved me. Good day, sir."

Col. Grady stood abruptly, snapped off a salute, and did an about face and walked toward the doors. They opened as soon as he got close and a secret service man in a black suit, sunglasses, and earwig were there holding it for him. Grady paused in the doorway and turned to the president. "Sir, I strongly advise you against ever sending men after the Jacksons. No matter what you think they may have done... You will rip the country apart if you do."

"That is all, Mr. Grady," the president said, no longer using his rank. "Please escort Mr. Grady to his quarters and put him under house arrest."

The secret service agent nodded and pulled a pistol from a shoulder holster and held it gently by his side. Grady grinned at the man, tempted to pinch his cheeks or put a wet thumb in the middle of the man's sunglasses. He was happy to still be alive. House arrest for essentially doing what was asked of him... he could deal with that. He knew he had enough support in the background that his men wouldn't let him stay here long. He just had to be ready when it happened. Nothing specific had been planned for this as it was more of an 'always be ready', and he would be. He knew of an old World War II bunker in Tennessee that had been decommissioned. Quietly and without approval, he'd had it brought back to readiness and stocked from the vast reserves of supplies. Only the chaos of the EMP had allowed his virtual theft of goods and supplies make a perfect bolthole and bugout.

If the Chinese went nuclear on America, he'd at least be safe for a while with enough supplies to keep him and those loyal to him safe for some time. Not in comfort, per se, but alive and healthy.

10

—————

"Change of plans," John said, his ear to the speaker.

"What is it?" Tex asked, hobbling to the truck John was half sitting in.

"Somebody hit the FEMA camp thirty miles north of us. Massive NATO and DHS causalities. They were ordered to bug out and head south, leaving the people behind who weren't loyal."

"Do you think it was somebody doing what we were working on before the Caliphate came to America?" Michael asked, referring to them breaking people out of the camps.

"Yes," John said, "by the sound of it. Apparently, a local sheriff escaped with his men and some materials and then hit some sort of research center. They are suffering severe causalities. I have a new plan, and I think you're going to like it..."

—————

"Sir, I mean John," Sgt. Smith stuttered, "you want me to do *what*?"

"I want you to hit the convoy in the front and middle. We're going to slip in using Michael's APC. It'll be tight quarters, but in the confusion, a NATO APC with DHS will look logical. With all the new men coming to the base, I'm sure their records are FUBAR'd. We can get in and do what we need to do and slip out."

"What exactly is the mission?" Tex asked.

Once the morphine had worn off and he'd had a day or two to heal, he'd woken up stiff but ready to join in the battle. The group's original plan had been to infiltrate, set up a diversion, and let in a special forces team to cause havoc and blow the lid off the place with enough proof to force the president to act. Even though John knew from Sgt. Smith that the president was aware of Hassan's betrayal, he'd not done more than give the stand down order. He wasn't actively calling on which units had stood down or not. They, the DHS, were just sitting and waiting. Something big had happened or was happening, and nobody at the Homestead could make it out. Sandra couldn't get through to her contact within the president's inner circle.

"Slip in, get proof. We already know this bunch is dirty. King and I will do what we do best. The rest of our teams are fire support. Sgt. Smith will be hitting incoming vehicles from afar, and shelling anybody fleeing when we start the fire inside."

"We're literally setting things on fire?" Michael asked.

"Naw, I have a feeling that there're supplies in that bunker that we'll want to keep away from the New Caliphate. If we have to use fire to destroy it, we will... but I think it'd be of better use for the folks we have coming in behind us."

"Behind us? Sugar, what the heck are you talking about?" Caitlin asked.

"One way or another, there's going to be a big push. Sandra's been organizing it for a month now. They're sweeping in from the southwest, cutting off supply lines and picking off stragglers from the bombing run—"

"Wait, you haven't filled us all in," King interrupted.

John had been on the horn nonstop, hardly taking a break. His mind was going a thousand miles an hour, and he had lost track of what he'd conveyed. He took a deep breath, and Tex pulled a Thermos out from behind his back and unscrewed the top lid. The scent of coffee immediately got everyone's attention and all the side chatter came to a dead stop.

"How did you…"

"Sugar, I'll love you forever if you share," Caitlin cooed.

"I haven't had a cuppa in—"

"How much is there?" somebody asked out of Michael's sight.

Tex just shrugged and reached inside the truck John was half sitting in and got John's mug out. It had the dried remains of the tea he'd found; they'd been without coffee for weeks now. Tex had been holding out on them, but John couldn't figure out how. His eyes were wide, and he saw Tex pour him a mug and hand it to him.

"I know I'm supposed to take 'er easy cuz I'm on the mend and all, but you haven't hardly slept. You drink this here rocket fuel, collect your thoughts, and lay it all out on us."

Hungry eyes watched the mug as John held it to his lips and took a long sip. He winced at the heat, but he could feel his synapses start firing smoothly. His brain had been feeling like a Chevy 350 that was running on five cylinders.

He didn't stop until over half the cup was gone, and Tex topped his cup off before turning to the crowd and started drinking out of his Thermos directly.

"Oh man," Michael whined.

"He ain't brushed his teeth this month," King groused.

"Mine," Caitlin said pulling the thermos from Tex's surprised hands and took a sip herself.

Angry words were shouted at the three of them due to the liquid brain power that was being partaken of, and Sgt. Smith walked into the middle of the commotion with a confused look on his face.

"What's the big deal? I brought like fifty pounds of ground coffee from the Homestead. The machines are set up near where our artillery FO..."

"Where are they all going?" Michael asked as the mob took off at a dead run.

King shrugged.

"I thought you were going to brief all of them fools," Tex said with a slight grin.

"Once they get them some java. We'll all feel better."

"APC 54376, WHERE ARE YOU COMING FROM?" THE VOICE crackled over the open line the DHS had been using.

"I wish we had Henrikas with us," Michael grumped to King. They had the APC absolutely loaded to the gills with John's spec ops folks including Caitlin and Tex, who had a jaw full of chewing tobacco.

"Bugging out. Was attacked by artillery and APC/Tank heavy weapons fire," King said.

"Who's your unit commander? Which NATO command you with?" the voice asked.

They must have put eyes to the markings on their APC as they joined the fleeing convoy.

"Sir, my unit commander is—"

The lead portion of the convoy disintegrated as several artillery shells and mortar rounds started hitting the convey.

Shouts over the frequency between vehicles were overlapping each other, and every vehicle, DHS, and NATO started going off-road and through the fields in evasive maneuvers so they could avoid any incoming and see any obstacles that the convoy had been blocking sight of. Michael was following several NATO-marked Russian Surplus APCs similar to theirs when the vehicle in front of him was hit directly. The explosion rocked the APC, bringing it to a dead stop as the overpressure almost flipped the APC. It came down on all tires, throwing people inside around.

"Oops," Smith's voice came out of John's tactical radio, and John cursed him without transmitting.

The bombardment stopped, and the remaining vehicles left the burning ones where they were. The survivors were starting to get to their feet. Some had fled the vehicles that had been flipped, but some vehicles hadn't taken direct hits, so injured fled the APCs and burning hummers disabled by the artillery.

"Slow," King said pointing to a group of three men who were standing shell-shocked next to a burning Hummer.

Michael shot him a confused look but slowed down to a literal crawl, making the vehicle behind him touch his air horn in frustration.

"Get on," King yelled.

Despite his shout, everybody's ears were ringing, and Michael could taste the coppery flavor of blood in the back of his throat from being so close to the explosion. These men weren't in anything armored directly, just a hardened off Hummer. Still... One of the men who was less shell-shocked than the others pointed and yelled to the APC. Three bloodied men climbed onto the outer steps, and the one who had given the orders got on top, near the turret and top hatch.

"I'll go talk to him," King said.

"Opsec," John screamed at King.

"I'm improvising. Door key," he said, pointing straight up.

King pushed his way through the bodies of men who were dressed as the DHS and to the hatch. He turned the handle and, being mindful not to fling somebody off, started lifting it slowly in case somebody was sitting on it. A surprised face filled the opening, the man who had gotten his men moving. Half of his left ear was gone, and a gash opened up over his right eye... The man was half blinded by his own bleeding, yet there was an intelligence in his eyes that let King know he was still in the game. He would have to be careful.

"I can't thank you enough," the man said, reaching a bloody hand inside.

King shook it.

"How bad are your men?" King asked, pulling open a pouch on his replacement vest and pulling a pack of bandages out.

"Concussed, cut. I was lucky, I was thrown out and just got a couple of nicks."

"You lost half an ear," King said pressing the bandages in his hand. "Half those on your left ear. No, your LEFT," he almost shouted, and the man nodded and complied.

King took two steps and got part of his shoulders and

upper body through the hatch. The man sat down, holding onto the turret for support.

"You guys saved our asses. Nobody else stopped. You have room in there for us?" he asked.

"No, you weren't the only ones we picked up. They call me King," he said, looking at the other two men.

"Swanson," the man replied.

One was barely conscious, the other was holding onto a handle near the edge, his lower body over the side. King noted he must have gotten onto one of the steps and was hanging on. The man had wounds all over his upper torso and head. Shrapnel. King pulled himself out and waved off the first man who had one hand clamped over his ear and made it to where the DHS man dangled off the side. He tried to anticipate the movements of the heavy APC, but it was still bumpy. The man he was looking down on was turning paler by the moment and was sweating profusely. King got on his knees and grabbed one of the handles on top and reached down with one large arm.

Grabbing the DHS man by the belt, he hauled him up one handed so swiftly that the agent forgot to let go of his handgrip and landed in a heap in front of King.

"Whoa, fella," he heard the other Agent say, "I don't know if he can take being manhandled like that—"

His words cut off as the APC ran over something and everyone on top bounced, King included.

"He can't survive falling off and under the wheels. Help me check him out."

"Thanks," the barely conscious agent mumbled.

They worked in silence, though the sound of vehicles and the crunch of tires and wind was near deafening. As King finished tying off a tight bandage on the man's upper arm, John popped his head up out of the hatch.

"King, the driver needs you," he shouted, and dropped back in.

King grunted, knowing that John was on a wanted list and hoped he hadn't just given away their ruse.

"Be right there," King shouted back.

"You sure you don't have any room?" Swanson asked, pulling the bandage aside to see if the blood had started clotting.

"Not once I'm in, sorry."

"No worries. You aren't regulars from around here, are you?" Swanson asked him as King started wiggling his lower torso into the hatch.

"No. Lucky we caught up with your convoy. Our group was getting slaughtered," he said hesitating heading all the way back inside.

"There's a lot of that happening. Us agents have to stick together."

"That we do," King said in his customary manner, short on words, long on meaning. "I'll leave the hatch unlocked. Have to close it so we can hear comms and the driver. You or your men need something, open it and give a shout."

Swanson nodded, and King climbed in and shut the hatch. He didn't lock it, but pointed up and held a finger to his lips. The team nodded, and the big man moved forward to where Michael was, bumping his way through the crowd.

"What's up, kid?" he asked.

"Oh nothing, just getting to the gates of Mordor. How do we get through?" Michael asked.

"Mordor?" John asked, puzzled.

"Lord of the Rings," King told him, "I told you guys, I got me a gate key." He pointed up.

"Well, we have about two minutes until we reach the

gate. They are reading numbers off the vehicles. We didn't plan for that," Michael said, a bit of worry in his tone.

"I told you, gate key." King pointed up again.

"Okay, man. Just have somebody be ready on the main gun." Michael looked worried, but his eyes never left the viewing slots and the bank of gauges in front of him.

"You know it. Caitlin's got it," John answered.

"Well hold onto your butts, here we go," Michael said. "Anybody want to go out up top and talk to the guards?"

"I got this," King rumbled.

King made his way toward the back. Michael shot John a look over his shoulder and then turned back to the driving. Without looking up, he asked, "What do you think he means about a door key?"

"The folks we picked up. He must have seen something or made a darn good guess," John said.

"I hope so," Tex said, "cuz bumping into everyone inside here is a pain in my—"

"Here we go," Michael said, and the inside of the APC went quiet as everyone waited.

Michael pulled the APC up to the checkpoint. From this angle, the hidden bunker wasn't visible, just the guard shack, an electrified fence topped with triple strands of razor wire and warning signs of an electric fence. There was a ten foot gap between that and a second fence that was only slightly less imposing. During their watch, they knew that the middle between the fences was often patrolled by dog handlers, and sometimes just the German Shepherds ran the gaps.

"Turn it off," a guard yelled toward Michael, who he could see through the slits.

Michael shook his head and heard King's voice over the big twin diesels.

"He turns it off it won't start back up," he all but shouted, his deep baritone carrying despite the noise inside and out.

"Your APC isn't on our list," one of the four guards screamed back.

Each of the four guards had an M4 on a drop sling, with a black pistol holstered at their hips. Three of them had their rifles at the low ready, but the man in charge was holding a clipboard. *The man in charge always had a clipboard*, King mused.

"They're with us," Swanson's voice was weak. "They were fleeing another major attack when they had the misfortune to run into the same ambush me and my men did."

"Swanson? Is that you?" The man with the clipboard looked up toward the APC's roof.

"Yeah, cuz, and I've got wounded. This is Agent King here, the guy whose crew pulled our fat out of the fire."

"What happened?" the man in charge asked and winced as somebody further back in the line hit the air horn.

"I don't know. I think it was artillery, but it could have been... heck, no it couldn't have been a bombing run, the folks with radar said there was nothing on screen."

"Artillery is more likely. How many wounded do you have?" Clipboard asked.

"Three up top," King said. "Mostly banged up and bruised inside."

"Regs say I have to throw this up the chain of command—"

Swanson coughed. "Cuz, I need to get my men to the medics. You can throw whatever you want up whatever orifice you have open. No offense. But... We're heading to the infirmary."

With a sigh, the agent started writing on the clipboard. "I guess you lost your vehicle, Swanson?"

"Duh... took an indirect hit, flipped it."

"Okay, then I'm giving this APC your spot. If it's going to have a hard time starting, make sure to park near the end of the lot where we can tow it out easier. We don't have spare parts for all this Russian rolling rust."

"Just a cranky diesel," King shouted. "Out of synch with the second one. Probably water in the lines."

The man nodded and waved at them to move forward with his clipboard. King dropped in, almost bowling over Caitlin. He put out a big hand to keep her from bouncing off the interior of the APC and then strode forward.

"That's it?" Michael asked when King got behind him.

"Door Key," King said pointing up.

"That's what he meant," John said, faux whispering to Michael, pointing up.

"No kidding."

11

"Seriously? The president was going to send you all the way out here to tell me that? Over."

Blake grinned and pressed the transmit button. "Yeah. My wife says it's simple psychology, and if you have partial power to make life much easier, you can get the refrigeration going. Once you get food storage up and running on a big scale, you have something to trade for more labor. People want to feel valued, and don't mind hard work. That's one thing I've learned since America went belly up... but if you force them to the water trough, you'd have to drown them to get them to drink."

Washington State's Governor, Isiah Starke, chuckled over the open air.

"That's the truth. When Franklin got in touch with me, he gave me a basic rundown. In truth, I was going to do something like this myself if I didn't have a mandate from DC that forced Director Atchley and me to do things his way. Yours has been implemented and tweaked. How was the response from the east coast?"

"Hesitant, resistant at first. Once they tried it, though..."

"It's just plain common sense. I think a lack of that has fouled us up some. I've met the president, knew him back when he was a common rabble-rouser... He has big dreams, and I think his heart is in the right place, but that good old boy is opinionated, and the opinion he likes to hear is his own. Over."

"Yeah, I've not had the pleasure myself, but I know he's not fond of me. I'm just going to avoid him for as long as I can. Safer for me that way. Over."

"Too right. Listen, do you have an idea for cold weather preparedness that you're going to be talking about on Rebel Radio? The reason I'm asking is winter is coming, and we've already had deaths from people trying to cook indoors with improper venting, fires, things like that?"

"I hadn't planned on doing it directly, but I figured it'd come up soon..."

"If you could, I'd appreciate it. I'd hate to lose half or more of the survivors this winter," the governor said.

"Why don't *you* tell them, especially if your biggest populations live on or near the camps currently?" Blake asked.

"Because, Blake, you're the anti-establishment, and I'm considered... the man. Fight the power."

Lisa was walking by, and she snickered. Blake shot her a look and grinned. His mother-in-law had surprised them all by definitely fitting the profile of a young grandma. She knew more rock and roll than most and was teaching food storage one day, dance the next... all the while helping corral the kids, keep Duncan from eating the bad foods and she had a wicked sense of humor.

"Fight the power," she said and started humming something.

She walked away before Blake or Sandra could make out what song it was.

"So you're saying it'll be more legitimate if it comes from me?" Blake asked.

"Exactly. Oh, uh over."

"I forget to do that all the time. Over," Blake said.

"Have you been in touch with neighboring states?" the governor asked.

"Not yet. Trying to work out the schedules and timing. Over."

"I'll work on what you shared with me, Blake, and if I can, I'll share info with Governor Scranton. Over."

"Thank you, sir," Blake said, "and if you need me to talk you through any of the changes during implementation just give me a ring. Blake out."

"Blake out," Duncan said in a falsetto voice and both Patty, Lisa, and Chris busted up laughing.

"Thanks a lot, Dad," Blake said good-naturedly.

"Any time," Duncan said. "Who's running the communal kitchen tonight?"

"Sandra and her squad were going to, but they got called away. Looks like half the Homestead has gone off to get some gear that Grady was going to drop for her."

"But they left hours ago," Lisa said, coming up from the basement with a handful of books.

"I don't know much. She took the radio call and left. I wasn't around for the first one, but I guess she got confirmation that supplies were inbound."

"She'd normally tell me if she was mobilizing something this big. I wish we had Smith around."

Blake understood that sentiment; Sgt. Smith had become the defacto third or fourth in charge around the Homestead. Blake had underestimated how much the soldier had been doing for him until his company had up and left to support Michael and King's operation to get proof of the government's collusion with the Caliphate, or to exonerate the current administration. Everyone had been playing things close to the vest, even Blake's wife Sandra who'd suddenly wanted to keep him close. He didn't mind, but for a woman who was virtually fearless, she suddenly seemed to be worrying. That almost sent Blake into the screaming meemies.

"I've been listening to the radio chatter," Patty said. "There're half a dozen planes that made the drop. As the last one was shoving cargo out the door, they all got recalled. They told whoever it was they'd already made the drops. Were ordered to fly in radio silence until the drops were made."

"Why were they recalled?" Lisa asked.

"Yeah, I'm wondering that myself," Duncan said.

"Maybe it has something to do with the cargo?" Blake asked.

"They didn't say what it was," David interjected, "but whoever was on the other end didn't use regular radio protocol at first. That's why the last pilot made the drop. Whoever called didn't have proper authentication, and they resorted to code words."

"That's strange. I wonder why they did that?"

"She'll fill us in soon enough," Blake said. "Chris, come on, let's go get a big cook fire going near the barn. Looks like you, me and the midget squad gets the dinner works going today!"

"Ooooh, that sounds good, Dad! Can I go tell Keeley?"

"Go ahead," Blake said, watching as his adopted son tore out of the house with a full head of steam.

Everyone winced when the heavy door slammed shut on

the spring, but there were smiles all around. They had felt safe at the Homestead for a long time. With the buildup of regular and voluntary militia forces, it'd be suicidal for anybody to attack the Homestead in force.

"Hey, Duncan, Sandra's on scramble, she wants you to go to the private channel," David said just as Blake was walking out behind Chris.

Blake paused and watched Duncan grab the portable handset.

"Hey, pumpkin, what's up?" he said after fumbling with buttons for a minute.

"No ears, Daddy, over." Sandra's voice came out of the radio.

"Let me know," Blake said pointing to Duncan who gave him the nod, and Blake went out to start the cook fire.

"You are going to seriously teach us how to start a fire?" Keeley asked, pushing Jason who was next to her, so he'd give her a little more breathing room.

"Well, I wanted to see how many different ways we could come up with. I've got lighters and matches - but let's say I didn't."

"Let's say you did. I'm hungry, and it's going to take a while to cook the stew," Keeley said in a sulky whine.

"Okay, so without matches and lighters, how can you start a fire?"

The kids grumbled, and Jason raised his hand. Blake nodded to him.

"Well, I saw on YouTube that you can use batteries, steel wool, paperclips and a whole bunch of other stuff."

"That's good! Listen though, bud, batteries are all going

to lose their power soon. Unless we get the power back on, let's not count on them. What else you got?"

A little girl wearing glasses raised her hand.

"Amanda is it?" Blake asked, and she nodded, trembling with nerves as everyone turned to her.

She had to be about eight or nine by Blake's guess. She was one of the orphans who'd come to live with them after the women and children had been rescued by the slavers during the early events. She'd not often talked and had only just started coming to Blake's classes. She'd been scared of all men after her ordeals.

She nodded and walked toward and pulled off her glasses, handing them to him.

"Yes, that works nicely! Where did you learn it?" he asked her, and she just shrugged her shoulders, staring at her feet.

"Did you read Lord of the Flies?" Blake asked, and Amanda looked up.

Despite not wearing her glasses, she met Blake's gaze and gave him a grin and nodded.

"That's how she says yes, Dad," Chris said.

Blake grinned and knelt down and showed the kids how to start a fire using the glasses, explaining you could also use a magnifying glass to greater effect or a pop bottle full of water and even a Ziploc bag full of water if they had the time to play with it. It took less than a minute for the flames to start building, and each of the kids did their part to break sticks for tinder and feed the fire until it was going well. Keeley started busting up bigger chunks, and Jason did a little showing off by dragging logs up for the littler kids to sit on.

They had previously fashioned a large rotisserie setup

out of steel rod and rebar from the diminishing junk pile inside the garage, but this time, it was being used to hold a large chunk of steel pipe. The middle had been bent in from having heavy cast iron cookpots hanging over it, and several hooks made out of rebar of different length were always near the cooking pit. Cooking for everyone usually meant the fire was manned all the time, but with Sgt. Smith's group gone it hadn't been as difficult. Blake knew it would be less than a week till the entire group was home, but he knew there was a small contingent due later on today with supplies that had been dropped in near Michael and King's positions.

Together, Jason and Keeley brought over the cast iron cauldron that had been scavenged, scraped clean, and re-seasoned after it'd been found rusting in an old livestock barn. Now, it was almost always used for the larger meals. Stews were the easiest for large groups of people, and Blake was going to let the kids do this tonight, with a little oversight.

"Why you put it down so low?" Chris asked Keeley.

"It's hotter down here right now. When it starts to boil, we'll get the mitts and use a shorter hook. That way we don't burn the dinner," she told him, grinning as he had his smile turned her way.

"But there is no water in it yet," he said looking back toward the hose that they hung up so the end didn't get in the dirt off the side of the rotisserie supports.

"What I found, squirt," Jason said, messing up Chris' hair with one hand and grabbing the hose, "is that the first water out of the hose is going to be hot or warm when it's been sitting in the sun. Then it gets cold fast. So if you know when to turn it off it's no big deal, but I'm hungry, and Keeley and I are going to cheat."

"Cheat? Like with Battleship where I look at your board?"

"Not cheating like that, but it's a trick to make the water boil faster. See, this pan can hold a lot of heat and a lot of cold. Right now, it's not really hot, so we are letting it warm up some before we put the water in. We'll add the hot hose water now while we're letting the big pot heat up."

Blake stood back, impressed. He'd seen Jason and his oldest brother who'd been working with Bobby, cook with the youngster before, but to see a kid who was twelve to thirteen doing this instead of obsessing about lost video games... Blake was happy and a little sad at the same time.

"Okay, I guess that makes sense," Chris said, though his voice conveyed a little skepticism.

"You'll see. Hey. What kind of stew are we making?" Jason asked, missing how Keeley had focused on how he was interacting with Chris.

Blake didn't miss it, and neither did the rest of the group. Making a mental note to talk to Keeley's family, the former blogger and homesteader just grinned and watched.

"Can we make a bacon and tater soup?" Chris asked hopefully.

Amanda shot up and walked to Chris. She was nodding enthusiastically and put an arm around the little boy's shoulders and looked at the only grownup nearby to see if it was okay.

"Not the sliced bacon, you want big chunks from the smoker I'm taking it?" Blake asked.

In truth, they had all kinds of pork stews and soups, but they'd yet to use any of the smoked meats in them. More because using the raw meat immediately saved on a step and time more than flavor.

"Oooh, I like that idea. I bet you we can add in some of

those wild carrots we dug up at the bottom of the hill," Keeley said.

The kids broke out into a loud discussion, and Blake sat down on a log, trying not to laugh as suddenly Jason and Keeley took over operations. Chris was sent to the smoker with Amanda to get a section that they'd indicated with their hands for size, and the other kids were running to get veggies from the root cellar and what they could pull fresh. When all the little ones were gone, Jason started filling the pot some more with water.

"You know, I think I found some wild leeks or onions near the old well," Keeley told Jason, "but I'm not for sure."

"You just bite them and try them," Jason told her.

"I don't want—"

"I'll get them. How much you want?"

"Double handful should do it for a big pot," Keeley said, wedging another log under the cauldron.

Jason took off toward the secret entrance/exit of the barracks, and Duncan came out and sat down on the log next to Blake.

"Good news?" Blake asked his father-in-law.

"Depends on who you're asking," Duncan said.

"Is it good news for us?" Blake asked him.

"Sandra's contact, Col. Grady, sent us a full complement of anti-aircraft batteries, missiles, radar, and shoulder-launched stingers and a ton of TOW wire-guided anti-tank missiles."

Blake stood up. Suddenly he wasn't sure if that was the good news or the bad news. The only reason they would send ordinance like that was either they thought that the Homestead was about to be attacked or that they would have to use it somewhere soon. Neither of which sat well with Blake.

"Is that the good news?" Blake asked.

"Actually no. That's just the news. Col. Grady was arrested after having the materials sent to us. He and those closest to him staged a breakout, and are now holed up somewhere. This all happened within the last twenty four hours. I guess the president thought Grady was arming us to either take over the government, or make us strong enough that we'd be on equal footing if they ever came after us."

"Why would they come after us?" Blake asked, dumbfounded, though he felt like he shouldn't have been.

"Because the president realized how much the rest of the people left alive in this country listen to you and your broadcasts."

Blake kicked rocks, looked at the fire, and then turned to see Keeley staring at him nodding.

"What?" he asked her, a little sharper than he intended.

"When you and Sandra were arrested, about every hillbilly from every holler from here to the Mississippi were on the radio trying to figure out where you were to bust you out."

Blake's mouth dropped open, and he looked to Duncan who nodded. "You knew that, Blake, they told you as much when you were at their COOP base."

"Yeah, but it's one thing to have a bureaucrat say it, than hear it from a kid..."

"Hey, I'm not a kid! In a couple years, I can get married, my family says."

"Oh yeah? Gonna rope you a Jason soon then, huh?" Blake teased, "You up for more weddings, Duncan?"

"Oh. My. Go— I mean... No," she said blushing at the near slip and the holy man sitting next to Blake.

"Sorry, I know I shouldn't tease, but that boy'd slather

himself in honey and run in front of a hungry bear if it meant keeping you safe."

"I know," she said, flushing crimson, "but I'm not ready for that."

"I'm teasing. I'll stop," he said and turned to Duncan to finish the conversation.

"Even though here we've only worked with folks some short months, you and Sandra are literally leading the nation through the dark times. Yes, you don't do it alone," he said holding up a hand to shush his son-in-law, "but you're the public figure, the voice. Half the people think you're MacGyver mixed with General Sherman, all rolled into one. They think Sandra is hell on wheels—"

"She is," Jason said startling everyone and handing Keeley what Blake saw to be wild onions, the dirt already knocked off the bottoms of most. "She was showing some of us some moves," he said and started doing a miniaturized kata, making Duncan bust up in a gale of laughter.

Blake and Keeley joined in, and when he realized they were laughing at him, he stopped, red faced.

"Sorry, I just like Karate stuff," he said sheepishly.

The two started pulling out pocket knives and trimming up the onions. With some prodding, Jason got Keeley to taste an onion. She made a face but started cutting them up and dropping them into the pot as the little ones swarmed back with more things to go in. Chris and his helper were both carrying a pork belly that had been in the smoker a day, nearly twice as much as had been asked for. Blake grinned.

"I sometimes think that this... the whole EMP business... Part of me wonders if this is how kids will remember things. The working and living together in harmony, or the bad times that shattered the world they knew before."

"Probably a little of both," Blake said after a moment, watching Chris hold up one end of the pork as Jason sawed through the middle with his belt knife.

"You want the bad news?" Duncan asked.

"No," Blake said, then after a moment, "Yes?"

"Sandra's fine, she's stashing materials and will be home soon... but that's not the bad news, I just didn't want you to worry."

Blake made a go on gesture.

"Right, so apparently the nuclear device came from North Korea, and yesterday, late in the day, the president retaliated," Duncan said in a whisper.

"How?" Blake asked, equally quietly.

"Let's just say that the only North Koreans left are those who were on boats, subs, or out of the country."

Blake cursed but stopped when Duncan slapped him on the chest. He'd drawn the stares of many of the kids.

"That's not the worst news," Duncan said leaning close, so nobody else heard him. "China wasn't happy. We used more than one device. Parts of China are going to be affected by the radiation and fallout. South Korea and Japan as well."

Blake tried to keep his face calm, but his worst fears had gotten worse.

"What do we do?" Blake asked the old soldier turned holy man.

"We wait for Sandra to come home. We pray," Duncan said.

"Does my breath smell?" Keeley said into Jason's face.

He scrunched up his nose and then leaned in and stole a kiss on the side of her mouth. Keeley's eyes opened in shock, and when she swung at the boy's head, he ducked and started to run.

"I thought you were trying to kiss me..." His voice floated over his shoulder as a furious Keeley chased him down the hill, promising vile deeds yet to happen to him.

"There's no way those two are going to have babies," Chris said in a serious tone, and the kids broke out into snickers.

"What are you teaching my grandson?" Duncan asked with a raised eyebrow.

"Nothing, I just told him that Jason likes Keeley."

"He likes her more than Legos!" Chris supplied.

"Ahhh, now I understand. Just remember, Chris, babies don't have babies. They have a lot of growing up to do. They can be good friends till they are old enough."

Chris looked around and walked over to Amanda. He hugged her close, and the startled girl looked down and hugged him back. Chris broke the embrace and looked up at the older girl. "Do you like Legos?"

12

"Hey," Michael said, bumping into John.

John whirled, his body tense. He relaxed when he saw it was Michael.

"Any luck?" John asked him.

"Yeah, there's four or more levels. They have the NATO troops and the unassigned agents, like us, up top here. Second level down is off limits to the irregular troops."

"What's the third level?" John asked.

"They said it's barracks for their regulars and those who've already been vetted. Whatever that means."

"There is a there a fourth level?" John whispered.

"Yeah, it's where they keep their generators, computers, and other stuff."

"Can we access the information from up here?" John asked.

"Caitlin is trying," King said coming up behind them. "No dice. Yet."

"Okay, so I'll stick close to you if you want King to go talk to his door key," Michael said, and King and John nodded.

King moved off, and Michael got close to John. Since the

government and DHS had been looking for John, he was taking extra precautions, but he was hiding right in the middle of them, in plain sight. The first few hours there everyone had been tense and nervous, but starting out at the infirmary had made things more or less easier. When the APC had been rocked by the artillery next to them, there were bumps and bruises, and like many others who had survived Smith's bombardment, there were bandages and artfully painted on bruises, compliments of Caitlin and Tex.

All of the vehicles were parked outside the big blast doors, and everyone had been directed in. With so many people coming in at once it was chaos, so after leaving the infirmary, John's group had an easy time meeting up and mixing in with the crowd of people. What they'd found was surprising in both a good way and bad way, as they'd spent the first two days interacting and creeping about the bunker. They were told that there had been an order to stand down and disarm, by order of the joint chiefs and the president. There were grumbles, but there were also rumors that John, Michael, and King had come here to find out for themselves. Was DHS working with the New Caliphate?

So far, they found it to be a no, but there were agents who were still wearing their crisp black uniforms instead of the navy blue sweats that everyone had been issued. Initial reports from folks there said the stand down order would be temporary and they'd be there for a week, maybe two at the outside. Nobody was happy with that, but Tex had suggested maybe they were vetting the agents who were on the first level to see if there were any to recruit, because the agents still in uniform were armed. Everyone else checked in their weapons at the armory near the infirmary on the first level, a large storage room with an even more impressive door than the fortified main door.

"Who's checked in?" John asked Michael quietly.

The young man had quit shaving for a few days and had some scruff on his face, and the lines around his eyes from everything he had seen had helped make him look years older than he was. His physique and outgoing nature had allowed him to blend in well, and he'd been working on befriending some of the black uniformed men. King had been doing much of the same, and Agent Swanson had taken a liking to the big man and had often joined him in the struggle to stay busy and not die of boredom.

"Tex, but he had to go back to the infirmary. I guess he caught an infection. Cut the stitches and pulled out a fragment. Cleaned up and taped his butt shut... er... anyway... Caitlin thinks she needs to be on a terminal connected to the mainframe here, or get into the communications room. The Kentucky Mafia is spreading out and just making friends, getting a feel for what people know."

"Any sign of some of our Caliphate friends?" John asked.

"Just once, heard somebody in the mess complaining about some of the guests' unusual dietary requirements. Food that has to be made separately and sent down to level three," Michael whispered back.

"Good. I got a chance to check out the elevators. Keycard access. Lowest level takes a special key as well. Unless we take out one of the black shirts, we're going to have to find another way."

"You have a plan, don't you?" Michael asked.

John smiled. "How limber are you?"

"Uh, what?"

MICHAEL SPENT THE REST OF THE DAY IN OR AROUND THE

mess. Since they were all new in the facility, they hadn't been assigned any work detail, but that didn't mean they wouldn't offer to help. As a matter of fact...

"Hey, sugar," Caitlin purred to the startled agent in charge of the mess, "can me and my cousin give y'all a hand? We're dying of boredom in here."

She'd artfully cut a v neck into her blue sweater, and the agent's eyes followed the curve of her neck down, and then his eyes shot back up to meet hers. He'd been caught, and he knew it. The agency had strict rules about sexual harassment, and suddenly he was remembering the other incident where HR had called him to the mat.

"I... Sure. Either of you work in a commercial kitchen before?"

"No, sir, uh... Agent Reynolds. I was a dishwasher when I was working my way through high school, though," Michael told him.

"I've done my fair share of short order cooking, hun," Caitlin said in a less sultry voice with a hint of anger. She wasn't going to let this agent off easy, though she'd planned this out because they'd observed him checking out all of the female agents already. "Momma owned a diner in Louisiana. It's in my blood."

Her story was mostly true. She had been a beauty pageant model in the Miss America contest, so in case anyone remembered her from years ago, she could go with what they may already know about her.

"Good. We're actually a little behind," the agent said, a little relieved though a little red on the ears and neck. "We've got some folks with special dietary restrictions. That means different utensils and pots and pans used. Different plates..."

"Like Kosher?" Michael asked. "I've dealt with that before in the restaurant biz."

"Same here. Just point us at something to do, or I might just die of boredom," she said with a big sigh.

Michael tried not to roll his eyes at Caitlin hamming it up a bit, but the agent was eating it up. The part of this he thought was dumb was the cousin bit. They had different accents, but maybe to this agent, all Southern accents sounded the same. Then he grinned as he realized cousins don't all have to live in the same state. Michael mentally kicked himself and followed the agent when he started walking.

They went into the back of the mess where four cooking surfaces were in operation, and there were two different three-tub sinks. Only one of them was manned, so Michael walked over to the unused one and grabbed a pair of rubber gloves that had been left on the side. The water had already been drawn, and it was still hot. All were labeled from left to right; wash, rinse, sanitize. Michael hadn't been fibbing when he told the agent he had done this before, so without a word to anybody else he rolled up his sweatshirt sleeves and jumped in.

Michael didn't pay attention as he attacked an insurmountable pile of dirty plates and cups, with more push carts full coming at somewhat regular intervals.

"I know you're not in here for the food," a feminine voice said.

Michael half turned as a beautiful agent in her mid-twenties bumped him in the hip. She had raven black hair mid-length down her back and had curves that most couldn't maintain with the short rations the rest of the country was living on. Michael knew he was in the middle of an enemy base but couldn't help but suck in his breath as she looked him in the eye. Green eyes, gold flecks. Michael never really... Well, the sheriff's daughter... but she was a girl. This was a woman, and she was looking at Michael the same way a dog looks at a side of beef.

"I uh... I heard that..."

"Oh no, cuz," Caitlin said from somewhere behind him, "don't you get backed up with them dishes, we got a lunch rush coming."

"The desserts are pretty good here," she told him smiling. "I'm Shannon."

"Oh, the desserts? Yeah. Honestly, though," Michael said, finding his brain and words again, "I was sort of dying of boredom."

"Oh? I was too. That's why I volunteered. That and there's way too many older men. They won't leave a girl alone, you know?"

Michael could believe it, and he shot a look over his shoulder. Caitlin was in front of one of the big griddles, a spatula in each hand. She was using her forearm to hold back the laughter, but he could see her upper body moving as the laughs escaped, if silently.

"I'm kinda new here," Michael said starting on another plate, but turning his head to the right so he could look at her. "We've been here a couple of days, and there's nothing for us to do until we get the stand down order revoked."

"I know, me too. I was just transferred to Little Rock when we were told to head north up here. Hey, what's your name?" Shannon asked suddenly.

Michael blushed and almost dropped the plate he was working on. He pulled off his right glove, getting his sweater soaking wet as he used his left arm and his side and held out his mostly shriveled hand to her.

"Michael. Sorry, my manners flew right out the window, ma'am."

"A man with manners?" she asked, taking his hand gently.

"Back to work, ladies," the agent they had volunteered to said as he came back through the swinging doors.

"Michael, what are you doing later on?" Shannon asked.

"After dinner, I'll be over by C block," he answered her truthfully.

"I'll look you up. It'd be nice to talk to somebody my own age," she told him giving him a quick look over.

Her gaze made Michael blush, and this time, Caitlin's laugh was joined by laughter from a couple of the men in the room as well.

"I'm looking forward to it," Michael said truthfully.

THE LUNCH RUSH OVER, CAITLIN WENT OVER TO HELP Michael with the last of the dishes. A few of the cooks and servers came by after Shannon left and gave him a pat on the shoulder and an atta boy. Michael wasn't used to any of this and was feeling conflicted. He was playing a part. He was supposed to be a special ops guy in training, but he was working the part. This was an act, just something to play until they could get to the—

"Hey, Miss Caitlin," the agent from earlier, Reynolds, came up with two pushcarts. Food steamed from beneath the metal lids. "Can you and your cousin get these carts on the dumbwaiter and send it down to three?"

Michael looked up and met Caitlin's eyes, and she just gave him a smile. Not the 10k watt smile she used to turn on the charm or make men's brains go to mush, but one that looked reluctant. Like saying "Sure, I volunteered, I stayed later than everyone, what's one more thing?"

"Sure thing," Michael told him.

"You can leave the rest of the cleanup for the regulars," Reynolds said. "Listen, I really appreciated the help today. We ended up short three more people. They didn't show up or check in today. I don't know what's happening, but that's the second time this month."

"Maybe they caught a bug?" Michael asked.

"Maybe. Listen, I don't have anything to pay you guys with…"

"Hey, we're all salary," Michael said and mentally winced.

Were DHS agents salary? Hourly? Did it even matter nowadays with the grid down and the country in ashes? Reynolds busted up, and soon Michael joined in with his laughter.

"Salary? Kid, I like you. Listen…" he fumbled in his pocket then looked around to see if anybody was looking, "…this is for the both of you."

He handed Michael a small baggie. The young warrior grinned and gave Reynolds a sly grin.

"If you don't smoke it, you can use it to trade. It's been the unofficial trade item here. Being the cook boss, folks hook me up so I don't give them slop. One of the perks of the job."

"Oh sugar," Caitlin said walking up and giving him a kiss. When she broke it off, she stepped back leaving one hand on his chest. "I'm sure we can make use of it. Can we come back later on for more?"

The agent looked a little stunned, and Michael knew he was, but in his mind, he knew she was doing what he was doing, playing a role.

"Yeah, you're welcome in my kitchen any time," Agent Reynolds said. "But I have to run. Staff meeting..."

He said it reluctantly, and Caitlin pursed her lips like she was sad. She gave him a small finger wave, and he almost walked into the doorjamb walking out backward. Once he was gone, Caitlin started giggling quietly and turned to Michael.

"That's how the game is played, hun," she said grinning still. "Good job on playing the bumbling virgin with Agent Shannon something."

"Um..." Michael said.

"Oh, she looped you with those big brown eyes?" she said taking the handles of a cart in her hands as Michael did the same.

"They were green with gold flecks," he mumbled. "Plus, I'm pretty sure she's eight or nine years older than me."

"You're smitten?"

Michael shrugged and focused on the end of the kitchen where two chromed doors with inset handles awaited them. Caitlin had checked it out when she had first come in and found that it was, in fact, the dumbwaiter, but they hadn't looked inside.

"I don't know. She made me feel hot and cold at the same time. I couldn't talk at first, it was like..."

"It's okay, it's what I do to get my own way," she said batting her eyelashes, but more as a joke. "Just make sure she isn't playing you. She came onto you pretty strong."

"Yeah, I've never been around aggressive women before," Michael admitted.

"Hun, you're so young you probably have and didn't realize it."

They pushed their carts in front of the door. Michael went and slid the doors to the sides. A gleaming stainless steel box stood there. It wasn't the size of a regular elevator, but it was almost five by five feet square. There were no controls on the inside, but rather on the side next to the door.

"We either go down with the food or one of us goes on top of the dumbwaiter and hopes for the best, right?"

"That one person would be me unless you know how to break into secure systems, sugar."

Michael looked at her, his head tilted.

"What do you think they recruited me for?"

"Um... Your loo—"

"Noo....... All you men are the same. Chauvinistic pigs,"

Michael started stuttering, and she laughed. "I was kidding ya, hun. Let's go. Caitlin backed into the chromed industrial sized dumbwaiter. Michael pushed his cart in straight and reached an arm out and hit the button for four. They were going to go for the mainframes first then to deliver the food...

There was a shudder, and the dumbwaiter started moving. Slowly. So slowly Michael was almost going to hit the button again when he realized that they were moving.

"Careful," Caitlin said.

Michael looked back and saw that she had her back to an open void behind her. A thick cable was within arm's reach. John had explained that if it was an elevator of any size, it'd have a counterweight somewhere. Since this wasn't a normal military base, they would have to figure things out.

"I am," he said, "this is just slower than I thought. Hey, that food smells good."

"Lamb Curry," Caitlin said, "Cooked it myself. Lots of good Halal food."

"Halal?" Michael asked.

"It's prepared and cooked for those who believe in the

Muslim faith," she whispered. "Now, I don't think we were supposed to ride these down, so if there is anybody waiting, we tell them we're new and we're volunteers."

"Yeah, as soon as the lights went out now that we're between floors that should have been a clue for most people."

"But we're just some dumb volunteers, and we don't know any better," Caitlin told him. "They can even check the records."

"Yeah, I really hope the records in the mainframes are better organized than things are upstairs."

"That would help," Caitlin said. "Shhhh... we're..."

They passed the second floor. The only way they could tell was the light that seeped in around the closed doors. They saw shadows along the bottom edges as they passed it and then as the roof of the cramped elevator was passed they heard somebody.

"Darn, must be for the muzzies. Smells good."

"Call up to the kitchen and have Reynolds get you some. You know how to get the good chow. He'll just get you some at dinner instead of lunch."

"I'm not even hungry, but that..."

The voices faded, and both of them let out a sigh.

"If we could hear them that easy..." Caitlin said.

"Yeah..."

THE FOURTH LEVEL WAS MUCH LIKE THE FIRST LEVEL, BUT empty of almost all personnel. In fact, when they first stepped off the elevator there was nobody nearby. The level was separated by two hallways. One of them had a black tinted glass with racks and racks of servers. The other had a quiet hum. Everything down there reeked of exhaust, ozone, and damp.

Two men walked out of a door on the left about twenty yards ahead but didn't give the two of them a second glance and walked down the hallway and went in another door. They were wearing the black DHS uniforms, but one of the agents was carrying a small toolbox and both had grease-stained hands.

"Let's get to the server room," Caitlin said quietly. "Remember, we're on three or we're lost."

"Got it," Michael said.

Acting like they were supposed to be there, they started walking down until they stopped outside a glass door that separated the hallway from the server room. Caitlin tried the handle and found it unlocked.

"Keep an eye out," she said and ducked in.

"So I'm just supposed to wait," Michael said to himself.

Through the glass he watched Caitlin move quickly. She ducked down a row of servers when somebody walked past at the far end, and emerged at the edge of Michael's sight. It was nerve wracking. He saw her fold down a keyboard from a tray and start typing. He watched for people and almost shouted out a warning when several people walked by. They paid no attention, and she kept going. After a moment, she pulled something from her pocket and put it in the computer. A USB drive, Michael knew. He was about to mentally do a fist pump when a voice startled him.

"Who's that for?"

Michael didn't literally jump out of his skin, but it was a close thing. It was one of the men from earlier who was standing on the other side of Caitlin's cart. He'd been so wrapped up in looking out for her that the man had walked up on him unseen and unheard.

"Food delivery from the kitchen. We don't know where we're supposed to take it."

"Well, what floor?"

"Third. It's the special Halal food."

"Damn, it smells good. You new here?" the man asked.

Michael was considering breaking the man's neck and stashing his body somewhere, when he saw the man wasn't armed.

"Yeah, we're with the group that came in under fire."

"I heard about that. Crazy stuff, man. Glad I got a noncombat job. Listen, though, you're going to get your ass wrote up or worse, this is the fourth floor. The elevators must be on the fritz again. Did it make you use a key to get down here?"

"No?" Michael said, cold sweat running down his back. "Just hit the button."

"Huh, I'll put it on my list... oh wow, would you look at that?"

The agent was pointing, oblivious that the wall was glass. Michael turned to see that Caitlin was walking toward them, a smile on her face. One hand was on her sweater, pulling it away from her chest back and forth to fan herself.

"Oh yeah..."

"That's what you were watching. I was wondering for a second. It was kinda suspicious but..."

"Hey, sugar, did you find out where we're supposed to be?" Caitlin asked Michael as she came out the door.

Her face was flushed, and a trickle of sweat was beaded at the side of her head. She brushed it away and looked at the man Michael had been talking to.

"Yeah, apparently I hit the wrong button on the elevator. We're on the fourth floor."

A mock look of horror filled Caitlin's face, and she

looked to the maintenance agent, "But we're not supposed to be able to—"

"It isn't the first time it's goofed up. Personally, I think they skimped when they built this shithole. Me and my crew are barely staying ahead of the repairs and maintenance. No worries, just get back on the main elevators and hit the button for the third floor. Easy peasy. Or you can send it up on the dumbwaiter."

Michael almost choked. This is where the narrative fell apart. Why didn't they just use the dumbwaiter?

"We couldn't get the one in the kitchen to work. Could you check it out for us? I don't want this food to get cold or go to waste."

"Yeah, sure!" he said, and Caitlin dropped Michael a wink when the agent turned to start striding toward the end of the hallway.

They followed him in silence. He got to the double doors, pulled them open, and pushed the carts in. He closed the doors and then hit the button to three.

"That's all there is to it," he said as they all heard the elevator moving up.

"Thanks," Michael said, "you saved us from getting our butts chewed."

"Yeah, no problem. Just head in there and hit one if you're heading back to the kitchen. It'll work without your card."

"Thanks," Caitlin said before Michael could slip up and say they didn't have one. "I appreciate it."

She pushed the up button, and the elevator door opened up with a ding. She stepped in, and Michael saw the maintenance man give her the once over and grin at Michael. Michael smiled back and stepped in, hitting the button.

"Hey, uh are you going to be busy later on? After dinner I'll—"

The elevator door closed before he could finish his sentence.

"Is it always like that with you?" Michael asked Caitlin.

"You know, it's a stereotype, but I wish I was born butt-ugly some days."

Michael looked at her and saw she wasn't kidding.

"Because the extra attention makes your job harder?" he asked.

She turned, and there was a tear rolling down the side of her cheek. "No, hun, cuz I'm more than a pretty face. I have a Masters in computer science and, even in the spec ops world, people don't take me seriously. Oooh, gotta protect the girl. Hun, I wouldn't wish this on anybody."

She wiped her cheek clear and sniffled.

"Sorry, I never thought that..."

"No, no it's okay. I just wish people would take me serious sometimes."

"I do," Michael said.

"Oh, not you. The world in general."

"You've never met Sandra, have you?" Michael asked her suddenly.

"No, but I hear she's hell on wheels."

"King trained her," Michael said grinning. "She'd come up to your shoulder, but from what the old man said, she knows more ways to kill an enemy than any operator alive. Even John."

Caitlin looked at him and saw he was being serious, "I've heard of her, but not much. I guess she got the whole white wash treatment so nobody knows if it's disinformation, fact or fiction."

"My point is nobody expects her to be a badass like you.

Not when she looks like one of the elf women in Lord of the Rings."

"She's really that tiny?" Caitlin asked.

"Petit, well, except the belly. She's preggers."

"When this is over, me and Tex..."

The door dinged open, and they walked out. They got a few curious looks from the black shirts, but there were so many people coming and going, they weren't stopped or questioned.

"So what did you do?" Michael asked Caitlin as they started walking toward C Block where they were bunked down.

"Set up our escape plan and got the info needed out."

"What about the Caliphate men?" Michael asked.

She held up three glass vials. They almost looked like perfume sample vials, but all were empty.

"What's that?" Michael asked quietly.

"What I did with the food. I was the cook, remember?"

"Poison?" Michael asked, a grin tugging the corner of his mouth.

"Botulinum toxin," Caitlin whispered back, "comes from eating bad food. If we're lucky, our getaway plan will take place long before the bodies are found."

Michael was smiling. By the sound of it, they could be out of this anthill in hours. Yes, they hadn't taken the base, but they had completed the mission. If the information was what Michael had hoped, it would force the federal government into action. He was about to say so when he turned a corner and saw Shannon sitting on his bunk. She was talking to somebody and, as he came all the way around, he saw that she was talking to King and John.

"Oh, there he is," Shannon said bouncing up to her feet.

"I came by to see if you wanted to go for a walk outside with me, see the sunset?"

Caitlin, John, and King were giving Michael an unreadable look, but King had a smile that was trying to break out of his permanent scowl. Still, he didn't look fully at ease.

"I'd love to. I have to talk to my boss, King here, real quick. Can I meet you somewhere?"

"Oh... Uh... sure!" she said her look going from confusion to a smile with a flush on her cheeks. "How about meet me by the sign for B block in the central corridor?"

"Sounds good!" Michael said, meaning it.

He watched as she bounded off and finally turned to see his three friends all grinning at him.

"Your cover must be pretty good, kid," John told him, pushing his shoulder.

"Yeah, at the end she hesitated, though."

"Here, kid," King said and pressed something into his hand.

He looked down to see a foil wrapper. When he realized what it was, he turned red himself.

"You pulled this out of your pocket to make her go away?" Michael chuckled, holding up the condom.

"Yup."

"You expecting to, uh..."

"Nope. Use those to waterproof detonation sticks for C4," King replied.

"Oh," Michael said, feeling dumb.

He had some in his personal pack for the same reason, but King had used the situation and what he had on hand to give them space to talk.

"So go take your walk in the twilight," Caitlin said pushing him on the shoulder. "And get to the APC when the alarms go off, and they start the evacuation."

Michael grinned and walked away, barely remembering to pocket the condom. He knew he wasn't going to use it. He didn't think they had long. They couldn't, because Michael remembered hearing about botulinum in school. It killed almost immediately. Maybe it would be better if he could get Shannon outside before the alarm went off. Caitlin, John, and King watched him leave, knowing that, good or bad, Cupid had shot his arrow. They all remembered their first and how helpless it was to go against the heart's demands.

"What did you do?" King asked Caitlin finally.

Caitlin laughed loudly. Loud enough that a sleeping Tex woke up three bunks down and swung his legs off the bed.

"What's going on, hun?" Tex asked.

"Nothing much, sugar, but we need to shuck and jive. I figure we have about an hour left in this lovely place."

=-The End-=

To be notified of new releases, please sign up for my mailing list at: http://eepurl.com/bghQbi

ABOUT THE AUTHOR

Boyd Craven III was born and raised in Michigan, an avid outdoorsman who's always loved to read and write from a young age. When he isn't working outside on the farm, or chasing a household of kids, he's sitting in his Lazy Boy, typing away.

You can find the rest of Boyd's books on Amazon & Select Book Stores.

boydcraven.com
boyd3@live.com

42383289R00064

Made in the USA
Middletown, DE
13 April 2019